Almighty

by

Lyn Miller LaCoursiere

Great Books and Novels
Minnesota Authors

Cover photo courtesy of Shutterstock

Cover design by Genny Kieley
& Lyn LaCoursiere

Format
by Genny Kieley

ISBN # 9781938990120

Almighty

An excerpt from Almighty

Jesse Ortega, a sixty-two year old, overweight and exhausted sheriff from Birch Lake, Minnesota has finally retired after several decades of stress and hard work 24/7. Now divorced from a cold hearted woman, he packs battered suitcases and heads south. And landing in Hilton Head, SC decides this is where he might stay. Only to find that while walking the beach, meeting beautiful women and finally feeling good, someone is out to kill him when rifle shots pierce the air and circle around his head. Is he destined to die now just after beginning to enjoy this new life he's carved out for himself?

Books by Lyn Miller LaCoursiere

Nightmares and Dreams

Tomorrow's Rain

Sunsets

Suddenly Summer

The Early Years

Silence

Moonbeams

Moonbeams Too

Almighty

From the Author

A famous man once wrote, "Shoot for the moon. Even if you miss you will land among the stars!" This is how I have tried to live my life. Back in the early days, before I ever got up enough courage to bring out my first book called Nightmares and Dreams, (I had the next three manuscripts hidden in my closet), I had drawn pictures of each of these four books with the title and my name on the cover and envisioned that's how they would look when someday they would become a reality! And, I was not a bit surprised a while back, when I ran across this same page and recalled the results of my positive expectations and recalled the day I had done this.

Someone else said, "Our most honest moments could be the ones in which we create fiction!" If so, I see that it means when I am creating a plot with people and places, situations and motives, I honestly, have to draw on my own thoughts and actions, my own realities, dreams and policies. (And of course embellish).

In Almighty, you'll meet Sheriff Jesse Montes Ortega again. He has been in all six Lindy Lewis Adventures, and also in Moonbeams and Moonbeams Too. And I decided now he needed his own story. So I hope this book will give you many hours of enjoyable reading late into the night.

I also want to thank all you faithful readers who constantly support my work. I love you all!

My books are available at Amazon.com in paperback and as kindle-books. They may be found at some Minneapolis stores and also at libraries around town. You can also get them on my website or you can contact me personally.

Regards always, Lyn

I wish to thank Jennifer and Danielle
for editing this book.
Mary M
again for her technical help.
Genny for her magical touch to
make this all a reality.

Also, thanks to my
Nightwriter friends for their
constant vigilance.
without which, perhaps I never
would have gotten that first book
out of the "closet"!

This book is
dedicated
to
Monica,
my friend!

-1-

The first few days of being at home, was a welcome relief from the constant need to deal with the problems of his constituents, but, after only a few of them, he was more than convinced this life was not for him. As retired, Sheriff Jesse Montes Ortega sat out on the patio with a cold beer and his wife's grating voice had found him yet again.

"Jesse, now that you don't have anything to do anymore, why don't you paint the house! I never did like this color."

He had stayed out there for several more hours and thought it through. He'd served out his term and he was done, and, done with the marriage to this nagging woman. Just done! That resolution made, he drank another beer.

The thing that had surprised him when he had told his wife he'd had it and was leaving she'd said, "Well, it's about time!" And, admitted she had wanted to leave the marriage years before but liked his good money making job. He remembered over the last few years that something was wrong when their love life had slowly ground down to zero, but honestly, he really wasn't interested enough to seek out the problem. But, it had seemed, she could hardly wait to contact a lawyer. Their son was grown, finished in college, and busy with his own life. He had told Jesse Junior he would send his new address when he decided where to land.

I gave that woman most of the money and the house. I have nothing left but my clothes in some beat up suitcases, he grumbled now days later as he drove, except for that nest egg which brought a smile to his face. Thinking back of his habit early on, of saving a few bucks from his paychecks over the years. His plan had been to surprise his wife with a bang-up vacation somewhere in Europe or Spain when they retired. Well, that had been a pipe dream. But now, he let his imagination go and with a small smile at the corner of his lips, he daydreamed of the possibilities with it.

He was driving his ten year old SUV on the road out of Birch Lake, Minnesota. Actually, he had no clear idea of where he was going, only foggy visions of somewhere south. So that was the direction in which he took off in.

Oh Lord, this feeling was magical. God almighty, he was only sixty-two and still virile. As he drove, it was the beginning of summer and he felt like an eighteen year old guy just starting out and driving off to a new city to seek his fortune. He turned on some "honky tonk" from Nashville and let the breeze from the open windows blow his salt and pepper curly hair around and sang to some of the oldies that he remembered.

As he neared the twin cities of Minneapolis and Saint Paul, Minnesota, he planned to stop for several days and shop and look around. Maybe have a drink with Mona and then Gina and Paul who were old friends that he had met through Reed. He was going to get a room in a nice hotel in Minneapolis for several days and take it easy, then start off.

Reed had suggested he check into Louie Lui's new hotel and check out some of the sumptuousness the place had to offer. And, when Jesse got there to check in, he found that Reed had already called and reserved a room for him.

"Mr. Ortega, your room is ready," a chic desk clerk said. "And Mr. Lui would like to meet you for a drink after you have settled in. Is four o'clock okay?"

Jesse grinned. "It's great. I'll be back here at four. Thank you!"

After he showered and changed clothes, he called down to their barber/beauty shop and asked to see a stylist for a haircut, and emerged an hour later with a suave new look that accentuated the sprinkling of gray at his temples. As he walked through the beautiful hotel he returned the interested looks he received from the female staff.

When Jesse shook hands with Louie later, Louie remarked, "I hear you've created quite a stir amongst my girls!" To which Jesse just grinned and shook his head.

"I'd like to have a talk with you," Louie offered. "That's if you have time."

"I have all the time in the world," Jesse replied. "And you have a beautiful place here." The two men walked down a wide hallway from the check-in area. The carpet was deep and plush in a soft coral with spectacular contemporary artwork by Georgia O'Keefe on the camel colored walls. Then they came into a bar, which was one of several and found stools at the bar to sit on.

"How long have you been open?" Jesse asked.

"It's been six months now, so things are starting to move along smoothly. This is my fourth hotel, but my first here in the US." Louie went on to say then asked, "What would you like to drink?"

After their cocktails arrived and more small talk, Louie surprised him when he went on to say, "Reed told me you have retired from Birch Lake, and may relocate. I've got a deal for you if you'd be interested."

Jesse's interest piqued as Louie went on. "I need a man whom I can trust, someone experienced in legalese, to take over as head of security, with the possibility of eventually taking charge of my other enterprises in the UK."

Jesse listened to the offer and was instantly impressed when Louie mentioned a starting salary.

"I realize you just retired and more than likely need time to rest." Louie went on to say. He was drinking Macallan scotch over ice.

Jesse took a minute to savor his beer from the frosted glass and glanced over the rich trappings of the room. His home in Birch had been quite large, and of course, decorated by an interior designer, but it didn't compare with the lavishness of this hotel.

For a minute, he wondered how he would like being in this environment, and especially working for someone else as he'd been his own boss for years now.

"Well Louie," he said and took a minute, "I need a few days here and more information before I can even think of making a decision."

"That's good Jesse, take your time. The man I've got is planning to relocate here in the US, but will stay on until his position is covered." Louie raised his glass again and took a healthy drink.

God almighty, Jesse thought, my plan is to travel south at a leisurely pace and enjoy the country. I'm not in any hurry to go to work again. But of course, this was a wonderful offer that he really needed to seriously think about.

"Louie," he said, "I would need to hear your expectations of the job."

"Sure." Louie asked, "Is tomorrow okay?"

"The morning okay?" Jesse wanted to know.

"Excellent. Stop in at my office when you get here." And they both stood and shook hands.

Jesse walked through the hotel and outside to a sunny day. Right away, he felt a change in the temperature here further south, as he walked downtown, as the warmth loosened up his stiff muscles. The fast traffic, honking horns and people hurrying about, also brought about a sense of excitement. Suddenly, the day opened up huge new avenues for him, both here and away.

His first plan was to shop for some new clothes at Neiman-Marcus. He needed several casual outfits and then some comfortable traveling clothes. He would then toss all his old baggy jeans and shirts and other old clothes out. The only thing he wanted to keep was a navy blue cashmere sport coat that he had worn for years, which he'd bought when he had turned forty.

In the store, he asked for a personal shopper to assist him. After the young man had taken measurements, checked sizes and listened to his wishes, Jesse was ushered into a small room where a tray of coffee and Danish rolls were set on a table, where soft music was playing.

"The morning paper is there for you as I will need about thirty minutes to start off with."

"Take your time," Jesse generously offered. Then he sat down and poured himself some coffee.

As he sat admiring the artwork and waiting for the coffee to cool enough to drink, his thoughts went back to Birch and his leaving the place he had spent the last number of decades in. He'd loved the brick rambler house with the extra rooms they had bought and where they'd raised their son. After all these years the basketball hoop that had been so popular was still out there on the garage.

He thought of his wife, or the ex as he already thought of her, although it had only been a week since they had decided to throw in the towel. Oh man, they'd been so in love those early years, and then the baby came. It seemed that even then their feelings for each other had begun to change. He'd been elected sheriff of Birch Lake County, which turned into a 24/7 job and she was busy spending his hard earned money. That was when he had started to tuck away a little at a time, to surprise her with later on.

As he sat there now, just a little loneliness trickled into his heart, at the big changes they had chosen to make.

Was it a good choice? He wondered. He leaned his head back on the soft back of the chair he sat in and let his thoughts wander randomly around in his head. Then the familiar scene came back again where he was in that place of constant sunshine, and that same faint image of the beautiful woman emerged to lead him away to that land of unbridled pleasantness. Could it happen? It only was a dream, but it really did give him enough courage to make the break in his life.

Then the personal shopper came into the room with an armload of clothes for him to try on. After several hours, Jesse purchased slacks and shirts and some accessories. It was now late in the afternoon, and he went back to his room to take a nap.

- 2 -

Jesse awoke at six o'clock in the morning as it was his usual habit. He never needed an alarm clock even if he had been up late the night before. This morning he had an appointment to meet with Louie Lui, the hotel owner, who had offered him the position of being in charge of security at this new enterprise. The idea had rolled around in Jesse's brain overnight, with countless questions. And after several hours into their meeting, in which Louie had spelled out his expectations, Jesse shook his hand again.

"Thank you Louie, it sounds like something I might be interested in down the line. But right now, I can't make a decision. I need time before I can truthfully do that."

"I understand totally," Louie agreed. "How much time do you need?"

Jesse didn't want to be tied down to anything or anyone and said, "Right now, all I can promise is I will contact you down the line and let you know how things are looking. My nerves are pretty shot."

"Fair enough Jesse, rest up." And that afternoon he loaded his SUV with his new wardrobe and tossed the rest of his things, suitcases and all, in a downtown Goodwill on his way out of Minneapolis. The afternoon was hazy as he headed south and soon was in the rolling hills of southern Minnesota.

Now he was really on his own and he loved it. In all the years living in the north he had never had the chance to see his own country, and, was surprised at the hills and valleys and the large farms still in operation. He'd grown up in North Dakota and Texas and had been hustled back and forth with his Latino family who was hired out to pick potatoes. He was the youngest of four kids where they all worked and only went to school when weather kept them out of the fields. His parents were Inez Montes and Gordo Ortega who followed their parents' footsteps of moving to where the works was. But Jesse's dream was when he became sixteen years old, he would take his GED test, which he did and passed. He had saved his money over the years and applied it to his college education.

As he drove, so many things were going through his thoughts he had to shake his head. Dam, he grumbled, this was not the time to rethink things, so he turned on some more music and instantly felt better.

The first night, he traveled as far as Chicago and stopped in a motel. The next day, the countryside in Illinois began to change and after another night of rest in Oklahoma, he was in the south. Now in Savannah, and about to cross the huge International Waterway Bridge that spanned far ahead over the sparkling waters of the Atlantic Ocean, Hilton Head Island, South Carolina, could be seen ahead. He inhaled the scent of the water as he cruised along.

His head swiveled from side to side gazing at the glorious pink azalea bushes that bordered sidewalks and boulevards everywhere. He recognized the kale plant from the gardens up north that was used here in the numerous flower beds. The whole area looked like a paradise, and what he needed now was a cold drink to savor it.

He stopped at a place called Shirlee's Café, that had a big sign outside advertising "Real drinks, fun times". A beautiful woman stood behind the bar and gave him a once over and a smile.

"Hello, and welcome to Hilton Head," she said.

Jesse had been alone in the car for days, and then too, he'd always had to tow the line living in a small town. But now for the first time, he felt a sudden wave of lust churn through his loins. He grinned and after settling on a stool at the bar gave her a once over as well.

"What's your pleasure?" she asked this time.

Jesse took a minute and asked for a cold beer. And within minutes she had placed a frosted bottle and a sparkling glass on the bar before him and poured.

Jesse took a deep swallow, then another and grinned. "Now that's a good beer!"

Shirlee stepped closer and leaned over. "It's called Millers Fort and it is my biggest seller," then added, "and it comes from my family's brewery!"

Jesse took another drink. "No kidding, you're from the Miller clan?"

"Yeah, born and raised way up there in the north."

As Shirlee talked, Jesse had time to admire her big blue eyes, long brunette hair and her golden tan, including what showed of her generous bust line. As she had bent over the cooler for his beer he'd had the pleasure of sizing up her lovely derriere as well.

"How did you ever land down here in Hilton Head?" Jesse asked.

It was going on four in the afternoon and Shirlee looked around the bar. Several singles were engrossed in a tennis match on a television otherwise the place was quiet, but would soon erupt into a noisy music filled nightclub after the busy dinner hours.

Shirlee poured herself a shot of tequila and downed it daintily, then smiled.

"I came down here several times, met a guy and tried marriage, and I've been here ever since."

"Well it's a good place then?" Jesse asked.

"The best," Shirlee smiled. "The people are easy to live with, the weather is great, and the tourist season is profitable."

-3-

Jesse found himself smiling and laughing with Shirlee and her friends who stopped in for drink. She introduced him as "another northerner who had escaped the ice age".

"Do you golf?" one guy asked.

"I did, but had to give it up when I couldn't fit it in too often in my days." Jesse commented. He saw the guys were all in shorts and had tanned legs.

"Jesse, come and join us and we'll get you going," another invited.

After several hours, he'd had his limit of alcohol and bid Shirlee and his new friends "adios" after promising to come again soon. He made his way down the one main street to the tip of the island to the

place he had called earlier and had made a reservation
with for a week.

The Beach Club was a huge complex that offered
all the niceties; there were private houses, condos and
apartments, where most of them faced out at the
scenic Atlantic Ocean. Several pools and numerous
tennis courts adorned the grounds as well. It had been
years since Jesse had seen an ocean and now he
looked forward to walking and seeing some marine
life. But he had to go shopping again and get the
proper clothes as he didn't own a pair of shorts or any
walking shoes for that matter. After he got the keys
and found his own condo he was delighted to see he
was on the first floor right next to the dunes and the
water. He dropped his suitcases and stepped out on
the balcony then stood breathless and inhaled the
island air. He sat down in one of the lounge chairs
and put his tired head against the padded back and
instantly fell asleep, and then into his dream.

*The beautiful woman smiled at him and took his
hand as they walked on a familiar beach.*

"Do you feel the magic in the air?" she asked.

*Jesse stood still for a moment. Something was
happening to him, but he wasn't sure what.*

*"Come on," she said, "you'll see." The cool
breeze blew her hair out of her face and now he saw
it was Shirlee, whom he had met earlier at her bar in
downtown Hilton Head.*

He was happy and the days were glorious with sun and fun as they frolicked amongst the islands and mountains. No clocks, no time cards and no responsibilities just the two of them together forever. He wondered then, was she the one in his daydreams who had been his playmate?

Was he in love or was he totally blitzed on booze? And then suddenly he awoke as the hot sun had put its mark on his face. He sat up momentarily disoriented and looked around at his surroundings and saw on his watch he had slept away a couple of hours. Evening was just about there and he was hungry. He grabbed his keys, locked up, and got back in his car.

Now he saw the Beach Club was situated next to a golf driving range, an outside shrimp bar, and a huge gas station. The whole area was filled with bamboo and assorted palm trees. Further on, a stretch of low land with aged water oaks laden with lacey moss grew on one side of the street and the other held an exclusive golf course. Jesse drove on checking out the numerous eateries until he came to one that looked interesting called Josie's. It was a white stucco building, totally covered with the national weed called kudzu, which grew over most of the south and could not be eradicated by hoe or ax, but only by a poisonous spray that was bad for your health. So it grew and multiplied almost overnight.

After parking under the palm trees, he walked up and took a seat in the shaded outside eating area. A bar leaned up against one wall and a small handful of customers sat on stools laughing and talking. Huge pots of flowers stood around separating the tables and the heady aroma from the pink azaleas bordering it, gave it character. The tantalizing smell of roasting meat had drawn him in and a waitress came over, wearing only a bikini. Jesse grinned.

"Now that's how to beat the heat," he remarked.

She laughed and said, "Hello and welcome". She set a frosted glass of water down for him and a menu. She looked to be in her late thirties, with a slim body and blond hair tied up in a pony-tail.

"Try the ribs this evening," she said, "The chef has just taken them off the grill, and, how about a cold beer?"

"That's it. All of it and I'm a happy man," Jesse said.

Julie was back with the beer in minutes, and as she walked away Jesse enjoyed the view. As he drank his beer the same new feeling came over him again. Each day it seemed to hit him again and again. Here he was, almost a single man, retired, had some bucks and looking to hang his hat somewhere new. God, like that saying went, 'life is like a bowl of cherries"!

Minutes later, Julie brought him a platter piled high with ribs, fries and toast, and a handful of paper napkins.

"Enjoy," she smiled and walked away again.

It apparently was after the dinner hour as the dining area was relatively empty.

But good jazzy music played and from time to time a few new customers came in.

Jesse took his time with his dinner and thoroughly enjoyed it as he hadn't taken time for much on the road. Now it all tasted like manna from heaven at this point.

After he had finished and had another beer, he asked Julie. "Where would you suggest I go to buy some shorts and flip flops?"

She looked him over briefly, at his expensive shirt and slacks. "You look like a Tommy Bahama man and there's a store just down the block."

"Thanks Julie." Jesse laid some bills on the table and stood to go saying, "I'll be back."

At the men's store he bought several pairs of shorts, some shirts and a pair of walkers as they were labeled. Back at his condo he changed into shorts, a tee-shirt and took off over the dunes and out to the water. He stood for a few moments and just gazed out at the huge panoramic view. There was no end to it, and hadn't he read somewhere that Morocco bordered on the opposite side?

He started walking and saw right away that there were numbered posts set in the dunes for emergency directions, and he was at fifty two. It was very quiet out there with only the waves making their own music. He met an assortment of people as he went on;

a lot of singles, some in bathing suits and some covered up. Older couples strolled along holding hands. Some folks were flying kites, and many were sitting alone peacefully reading. Others were gathered in groups visiting.

Evening soon approached and the populace began to leave. But Jesse walked on, deep in thought, swinging his arms and totally relaxed, breathing in the refreshing ocean air. However, on his walk several days later, a strange thing happened. He suddenly heard a popping noise, and then felt the air rush by his head. Startled, he recognized rifle shots. He instantly dropped to the ground and covered his head. Then another hissed by.

God almighty, he mumbled. What the hell was happening, right now when a whole new life was opening up for him?

-4-

Jesse Montes Ortega, retired sheriff and former resident of Birch Lake, Minnesota, had dropped down flat on his stomach on the beach of Hilton Head Island as another bullet hissed through the air. He lay perfectly still.

Danger swept through his body. But not moving a muscle, his thoughts were going a mile a minute. No one knew him here in this town! But someone was playing with him, as they had a clear shot at him and could have hit their mark. The big question was, who the hell was sending him a message?

After a good five minutes went by, he got pissed at being in this situation and jumped up and took off.

He was at post number sixty and had about a mile to get back to his place. He walked fast.

God almighty, the first thing he was going to do when he got back to his condo was take the .38 out of the suitcase. He needed to carry it again. That was if he got back in one piece!

There were not a lot of people out on the beach now and the sun was going down sending his long shadow out to the water's edge. As he walked, he studied the windows and balconies of the facing condos and apartments and could see numerous residents busily moving around in their homes.

Whoever was messing with him was a mystery! He'd put many lawbreakers in jail over his long stretch as sheriff, but couldn't place one that could connect with him here of all places.

Finally he got back to post #52 and hurried up the boardwalk and over the dunes to his condo. He noticed when he slipped the key into the lock on his door his hand shook and that pissed him off. When he got in he sat down and put his feet up on an ottoman. Now he wished he had some whiskey to soothe his nerves as he needed to think.

Should he contact the police department? Could it be there was a shooter loose in town taking pot shots at tourists? Someone pissed about some cock-eyed issue?

God almighty, he hadn't even been in Hilton Head one full week and here he had to deal with this crap again! He thought he had gotten away from all of this.

He was totally wiped out and got into bed, as he needed to sleep. The next morning after a shower and getting dressed, he was ready to find some breakfast. As he'd driven into town he had noticed a restaurant located right on Main Street called "The Diner". It had looked to be a popular place and he'd seen many out of state, late model Lexus and Caddies parked in and around. It was built to look like a box car and it had beautiful landscaping spread under the shading water oaks and palms. Inside, it had booths and tables and looked to be several car lengths long. A hostess sat him at a small table by a window and laid a menu down for him. After he chose a steak and eggs, he picked up a local paper that had lain nearby on a chair. It carried the usual array of items for the interested residents like advertising and obits and he put it down hurriedly when his food came. And he failed to see a small gossip item in the bottom of the last page that read, "Prominent families party at their own Greeley Plantation"!

The shooting episode last night on the beach was still uppermost in his mind as he ate. And today he would look up the police department and report the attempt on his life. Just in case the asshole gets his target next time, he thought with tongue in cheek.

The Hilton Head Police Department was located on the main street right next to a popular up-scale shopping center. He parked his SUV in the visitor's space and entered.

It was a one story white stucco building with a small landscaped front yard. Pink azalea bush's lent its blazing color to the lush green pines and ivy ground cover.

A young man in uniform sat at the desk right inside the door and looked up from his laptop as Jesse stepped in.

"I'd like to see the Chief please," Jesse proclaimed.

"Chief Anderson is tied up right now. Can I get your name and why you are here?"

Jesse looked at the fresh faced young man. "I've only got a few minutes. Name's Ortega and I'll tell the Chief what it's about."

The clerk looked pissed at this affront, and after fifteen minutes, he stood up and ushered Jesse in to the inner sanction of the department. A tall trim, good looking blond woman stood up and extended her hand.

"Mr. Ortega, I'm Chief Anderson, and I like to know ahead of time what my visitors want to see me about."

"Excuse me Chief; I apologize if I offended your guy out there." Her dark blue uniform fit her body in just the right places and Jesse found he had to tear his eyes away from her gorgeous legs.

"Jesse Ortega, Chief," he repeated. Then added, "But I must say I'm surprised to find someone like you in this office."

"Like me? What do you mean by that?" Chief Anderson asked defensively.

"I mean a good looking woman like you." Jesse had begun to sweat.

The Chief commented dryly, "I know, I surprise a lot of people."

Then to satisfy his curiosity he had to ask, "Have you been in office long?"

"Five years. My family has held this seat for several generations now. My dad and my grandfather before him, and I was the only kid in the family and a girl to boot, anyway, I inherited the role."

Now Jesse was glad he'd showered again and used some of his Armani cologne before leaving this morning.

"What can I do for you Mr. Ortega?" She asked.

"Call me Jesse, Chief. I'm from Birch Lake, a small town in northern Minnesota and just got here a few days ago. I'm a retired sheriff."

"Well," she smiled, "I'm always happy to meet someone in the same line of work. Congratulations on your retirement. Take a seat Jesse and tell me what I can do for you." Jesse sat and relaxed a bit and raised a foot over a knee. "Chief, last evening when I was out for a walk on the beach, someone fired three rifle shots, too close to me for comfort."

Her manner instantly changed to business. "Where, and what time?" She exclaimed.

"I'm staying at the Hilton Head Beach club and it happened when I was at beach post number sixty."

"I know you didn't call it in or I would have known. A big mistake Jesse, why not?" Her blue eyes bore into his.

"I thought about it, but I wanted to meet your department first."

"Good Lord, Jesse," she exclaimed again, "that's what I'm here for. If someone is shooting at our tourists, I need to know right away!"

"Sorry, Chief, and I can understand how you feel." He glanced admiringly at her outburst and even pissed off, she looked good. He checked her left hand for a ring but it was bare. Her nails were short and the only adornment she wore was a Rolex watch.

"How do you know it was a rifle?" She asked.

"I've fired and heard enough of them in my time to know Chief."

"Oh hell, call me Juel, Jesse, that's spelled J-u-e-l," she said then and leaned in closer and said, "We've got to get on this Jesse, and I've got an idea."

Jesse felt his heart ticking away a little faster than usual, and said, "I'm all yours!"

- 5-

Elle Moore stopped in the middle of the living room and clutched the fluffy robe tighter. It had rained earlier, a short summer shower that left a chill in the air. Just now, the evening sun had come out sending beams of light dancing around the room. She loved the beautiful furniture and accessories that came with her new house on the beach. There were two sitting areas here in the big room; one with a white and blue couch and white soft chairs, and the other with four light blue matching easy chairs surrounding a huge rectangular coffee table. Each area had a large wool rug over the honey colored wooden floors. One whole wall was covered with paintings, large and small, both contemporary and traditional themes. Artwork that should have been picked up before the closing sale.

"We're contacting the owner," the Hilton Head realtor had said as Elle was being shown around the home on the dunes just off the Atlantic Ocean.

The white stucco, rambler style house had everything when she moved in, such as beautiful copper pots and pans, Egyptian cotton linens and expensive knick-knacks.

Elle walked into her bedroom and then stopped in front of the full-length mirror. She looked so much like her mother now and stood lost in the past and remembered her mom's last years. Her transformation from an active socialite to a gentle grey-haired grandmother had been a change so gradual, so quiet, no one seemed to notice.

Hell, Elle said and stuck her tongue out at her reflection in the mirror. The tall, five foot seven blonde, looking back at her had a few lines in her face, some sagging here and there, but nothing too scary yet, she decided.

Not too bad for a broad in her fifties, she grinned and went into her bathroom and turned on the water. She looked over the array of bubble bath and oils and poured big slurps of perfumed essences in the water and watched the bubbles and oil mix. She loved this part of the house. It was lacey and feminine, and done in soft colors of daybreak. Pinks, mauves and creams were everywhere. From the drapes and bed coverings down to the furry mauve rugs scattered here and there on the honey-toned wood floor. Chaise lounges, covered in the same warm mauve hues were placed by the French doors that led out to a small patio.

The cool air conditioning in the big house gave her goose-bumps and she hurriedly stepped into the tub, and luxuriously sank down in the hot caressing oils and began to feel the rejuvenating softness soak in. She laid back, closed her eyes as she listened to the classical CD music coming over the sound system and let her thoughts ramble on. Tonight was a special night. A date with a man she had been introduced to by friends a few weeks ago, and had felt an attraction to. And after several conversations over the phone, he had asked her out to an evening of dinner and dancing. Now as Elle relaxed in her tub, she felt young and beautiful, and so excited about her first summer in her new home by the ocean in Hilton Head, South Carolina. And finally, away from the stress of the big city living in Savannah.

She hadn't noticed that the skies had fiercely clouded up again as suddenly, the music stopped and the room went black, totally without a trace of light anywhere.

She stiffened, suddenly terrified, as darkness enveloped her, as the silence was amplified with nothingness. Scared, unable to move, and unable to think, her cozy world turned into an unfamiliar place. Finally, she gripped the edge of the tub and eased herself out, accidentally bumping over a glass jar of bath salts that crashed loudly on the ceramic floor and sent splinters flying. She crawled on her hand and knees in the dark and found her robe, but small cuts covered her knees.

She sat there on the bathroom floor wondering what the hell to do. She remembered there was a flashlight in the kitchen cupboard, but that was a long way off in the dark house. All at once, her heart began to jam wildly against her ribs as she suddenly thought she felt a presence. Was someone in her house? She couldn't see or hear anyone, but her senses were screaming. She thought she could almost feel the vibrations of another living being.

As tremors of fear shuttered through her body, the seconds dragged. Then the lights suddenly flashed back on, with a brilliance that blinded her, and Montavoni's music sprang into action again on the sound system with a crash of cymbals. She looked franticly around her bathroom and saw nothing seemed disturbed. And after what had felt like hours of terror, the hands on the small clock standing on the sink had only moved a few minutes.

-6-

"Let's go into our conference room. No one will disturb us there." Juel Anderson, the Police Chief of Hilton Head, SC motioned for Jesse to follow her.

She led him into a large room with a table big enough to seat a dozen. "We have meetings in here when the public is invited," as she motioned him to a seat and took one next to him.

"Okay Jesse, start at the beginning. When you first came out to the beach, did you notice anyone acting strangely, or seeming to be interested in you?"

"You know I was so into the scenery, both the ocean and the scantily clad females I didn't really study anyone in particular."

"Did you notice anyone acting suspicious?"

"God almighty, after someone tried to kill me out there, everyone looked guilty to me as I got the hell out of there!"

"Do you still carry a gun Jesse?' She asked then.

"I still have one. It's legal."   Jesse answered defensively.

"I suggest you leave it in your suitcase and let us do our work," Juel Anderson advised.

"I understand your point Chief," Jesse agreed. But he had never before let someone else be entirely responsible for his safety.

"Jesse," she asked, "you did report this shooting episode to the security people at the condo office didn't you?" She sat back and ran a hand over her hair.

"Not yet," He said easily.

"What, you didn't?" She had an incredulous look on her face. "Why not?"

"I needed to think about this Chief, and maybe the shots weren't meant for me."   He didn't feel like saying he wanted to check out the effectiveness of the department first in this southern city.

"Sir," she said in a frosty voice, "I need to know about these things happening in my town. However, I don't want you to tell anyone shots were fired yet, we don't want the shooter to find out we're looking for him."

"Okay," Jesse said.

She was busy with her notes and then asked, "Jesse, what kind of cases did you have up there in Minnesota?"

"Oh hell, I gave out a lot of parking tickets," Jesse remarked easily.

"Really, I thought so, as you must have had an easy job up there in the boonies." She laughed then.

Jesse looked at her with tongue in cheek.

Chief Anderson went on to say. "Now Jesse, I want you to stay off the beach."

"Okay. And what are you going to do?" He asked.

"I'm going to have my people patrol that area and see what we come up with."

"Do you have much in the way of crime here?" Jesse wanted to know.

Chief Anderson smiled, "Like you, I give out a lot of parking tickets." And with that she got up signaling their time was over, but added, "Oh yes, and be sure and leave your cell number with my secretary."

Jesse walked out of the police department pissed and not at all confident of their efforts. He felt the chief had purposely been discourteous of his job and its area.

Before this asshole had started firing at him out there on the beach, Jesse had really liked the free and easy feel of the sun and sand, and the ocean breeze on his bare arms and legs in the wife beater t-shirts and shorts he wore. Back in his condo and dressed again in them it wouldn't be long before he was tanned and in shape. It had been decades since he'd worn anything like this as he'd always felt he needed to portray a "no nonsense image" to his people. He had to smile to himself now when he looked in the mirror at his image and thought of his soon to be ex-wife's horrified expression if she could see him now in this new look, flip-flops and all.

Not to be defeated in what could have been just a comedy of errors, he got in his SUV and headed to the other side of the island for another try at a walk in the sun. The only thing different about his attire was the .38 held securely in his short's waistband under his shirt.

Feeling invigorated after several miles, by now it was way past lunchtime. And after a stop at his condo for a shower and a change of attire, Jesse retraced his tracks back to Shirlee's Café. As he walked in the restaurant he saw another woman was manning the bar, and disappointed now, he asked for a beer.

"Coming right up," the bartender said. Just then, Shirlee came in looking like a million bucks; dressed in white jeans, a silver spangled shirt, white wedgies and silver earrings.

And not used to many women's pointed interest, Jesse's heart did a summersault when she smiled and said, "Hello Jesse, I was hoping you'd stop in again."

He grinned, "And I was hoping I'd run into you again."

"You can find me here pretty much every day."

"No time off?" Jesse asked.

"Sure, if I want it." Shirlee went behind the bar to the cash register apparently to check the sales.

"I see we had a busy lunch today?" She remarked to the bartender. "I'm here now so go and take a break and eat something." The young woman hurried away after smiling gratefully at her boss.

"That's Dani, a good friend and someone I can count on." Shirlee reached over for the coffee pot and poured herself a cup.

After taking a drink of his beer, Jesse ran a hand over his mustache and said, "We all need that special someone."

"I think men have a harder time getting close to each other." Shirlee commented and after checking with customers she came out around the bar and sat.

"Seems so and Jesse went on to say, "I have a couple."

"What line of work are they in?" She asked.

"Conners is a retired attorney, but takes on security cases from time to time for major companies. My friend, Ed owns a car business and is known all over the North country."

Shirlee had laid a rhinestone covered container on the bar and opened it for a cigarette and slipped it in a long elegant holder. When she saw Jesse looking at her and frowning, she smiled and said, "We don't have the same strict laws here, in the south."

"You don't? Well, then next time I'll bring my stogie along."

"I'm kidding Jesse, since its quiet in here I'm going to sit back and remember old times and enjoy a smoke again."

"I like a woman who knows how to enjoy life." He ran fingers over his mustache again in thought. He didn't see any rings on her left hand, but maybe it was too soon. Ah hell, what would a beautiful woman like her see in a backwoods old guy like him anyway?

"Is something wrong? Your face clouded up there for a minute." She asked then apparently noticing a frown cross his face.

"Nope, just liking your place and the company." Jesse said easily, and she smiled at him. "I've seen your ad, you're an entertainer too?" He asked then.

Shirlee laughed. "I had to do something to keep my customers here after their dinner so I started to play the piano and sing some of those oldies. Before I knew it, I had a piano bar."

"Really? I'm impressed." Jesse was feeling better now, and maybe they had something in common after all, because he loved his music. That was one thing he had taken from his home besides his clothes and that was his collections. He had every CD out by his favorite country artists, rock and roll performers and classical enthusiasts. He remembered how his soon to be ex-wife would yell at him to turn down that "God awful noise" coming from his "man cave" in the basement back in Birch when he had time to go there.

Then the realization hit him, right in the belly this time. He did not have a home any longer. Those four walls that he had loved and slaved to keep from falling down was not his any longer. He'd given it up. Shit, he thought and swiped his hand over his mustache and chin. But he took another drink of his beer and swallowed hard.

-7-

Elle Moore forced her stiff body up from the floor, slipped into the robe and tiptoed cautiously out of the bedroom and into the living room. Somewhat unsteady on her feet after the bizarre scare in the bathroom she brushed against one of the many paintings that covered the walls. A sharp pain pierced her shoulder from the edge of one of those oil paintings that had come with the house. She sucked in her breath, then stood stock still as her eyes locked on those of a picture of a joker in a large painting of red and orange outlined in black. He was staring at her and laughing. She didn't remember ever seeing this piece of art. And she ran out of the house clutching her cell phone and called 911.

"Hilton Head Police Department," a male voice said. "May I help you?"

"Someone is in my house," Ellie said as she zipped her robe and swiped her red hair off her face.

"May I have your name and address please?" He asked.

It all came out garbled.

"Slow down. Get out of there, then repeat that!"

Elle sucked in her breath and managed to give him the address as she ran. Her car stood right out on the drive and she scrambled in, and heard the locks click as she backed down onto the street swerving back and forth in her haste to get away.

After what seemed like eons of time a squad car finally flew into the driveway. "You're Elle Moore, the person who called?" An officer asked after coming to stand by to her car.

"Yes," she answered.

"You reported someone is in your house?" The officer asked looking at his notes.

Her voice came out in a whisper. "I was taking a bath and all the lights went out."

"What did you see?" He asked. To her he seemed to be too young to be an officer of the law. Only a kid, she thought.

"See? I didn't see anyone, but I could feel someone was there close by." Elle replied.

He cleared his throat. "Miss, I'm sure there's an explanation for this, there's a storm coming and that may have been why your lights flickered like that. But I've called for another squad and we'll check your house and grounds for you."

"Thank you," Elle replied feeling a bit safer now and just a little foolish as she started to doubt herself.

She stayed in her car with her doors locked and the motor running. Jesus, she whispered under her breath, she'd only been here in Hilton Head for a few months and had spent only a few days in her lovely new home.

After about fifteen minutes the two officers came back to her car and she opened the window again.

"We've searched every room thoroughly and the outside area. We didn't find or see anything that seemed strange. We think it's safe now Miss Moore. But you call us again if you need too," the older looking one said. And they left. But he shook his head in wonder and said to his partner "these city people move here for the peace and quiet of being lulled by the ocean, and then get spooked when it's too quiet."

Inside again now, but still shaken, Elle poured herself a brandy from the crystal decanter standing on the bar in the library and sat down. The wind had started to howl outside then from the oncoming storm, and branches brushed against the house and made eerie sounds. She sipped slowly and took the brandy along and walked back to her bedroom. On the way, she stopped to straighten the seemingly sinister picture. She frowned as she studied the vibrant colors of the face, the green painted hat with a bell hanging on its forehead and its ruffled collar. Glancing back then as she hurried down the hallway, she saw the eyes in the face of the joker seemed to be following her.

She just had to get away from this house for while tonight and decided if she hurried, she could still be ready for her date. And promptly at eight o'clock the doorbell chimed and Hamp stood there. Tonight they were going to the Blue Marina, a lovely supper club located right next to the ocean. Elle put on a black fitted dress, dark nylons and black snake skin shoes. Her red hair shimmered and diamond jewelry sparkled as she moved.

"Hello Elle," Hampton said as he stood there looking like someone out of a GQ magazine ad. White linen slacks and a white shirt complimented a blazing red jacket. Gucci shoes looked elegant on his bare tanned feet. His hair was sandy and shot with grey, and just enough to make him look sexy, and the crinkles around his eyes seemed to make his brown ones deeper. The only thing that showed his age could have been his gray mustache. Their colognes mixed as he stepped in and kissed her lightly on the cheek.

"You look lovely tonight," he said as he moved back for a better view. His eyes went over her slowly.

Suddenly feeling unnerved, Elle picked up her wrap and evening bag, and hurrying on outside ahead of him, she said, "And, I'm looking forward to a special night out."

-8-

Jesse stood at the bar in Shirlee's Café down on the ocean dunes and stroked his mustache. She had joined him for a drink as the place had an afternoon lull with just several customers in the place.

"How do you like our town so far?" She asked.

Of course he hadn't said anything to her about the rifle shots. "I think you've got a perfect setup here. Weather seems to be great, so right there it's a great draw."

"I do love it, Jesse. But we occasionally do have some hurricane storms that really scare me." She had been holding the cigarette in its holder and put it between her lips and held the lighter.

"Here, let me," Jesse exclaimed and took the lighter out of her hand. When she lowered her head to inhale, his hand shook suddenly.

If she noticed, she didn't mention it, and he had a moment of not being sure just how to explain it. He didn't want to say anything to her that he was still jittery about the shots at any rate.

"Do you have family here?" He asked then.

"No, not now, I have two daughters but they're both away busy with careers. One is in California, and the other in Mexico."

"Have you lived here long?" Jesse asked then.

Shirlee laughed. "Almost twenty years now. I remarried here after a few years and that fizzled out, but I stayed on and bought this place."

Jesse's thoughts brightened at her admission.

Several tables over, he didn't notice four ladies having cocktails and a lunch. And he didn't realize what a handsome picture he made standing at the bar. Jesse Ortega was a handsome Latin man in his early sixties. The last few months back home in Birch, the stress over his broken marriage, and then finishing up his career as a sheriff had been bittersweet and he had lost a lot of weight. Forty pounds right off his middle, and now his new clothes were several sizes smaller, and his sun darkened face just after a short time here on the sun kissed island, looked good next to his white shirt and his graying hair.

"Are you traveling alone?" Shirlee asked then.

"I am. I'm almost divorced too," he admitted with almost a grin breaking out over his face.

"Whatever made you come to this place," she wanted to know. "Do you know someone here or have you been here before?"

"No, I don't know a soul and I've never been here. But an acquaintance I knew up north talked about this island and it seemed like someplace I would find interesting."

"This place has a lot of history. For instance it's still possible to find spent gun shells in the sand on the beach from when the Germans invaded our coastline years ago back in WW II."

"I read about that," Jesse commented.

"Like I said, there's a lot to learn about this island." Shirlee blew smoke out over the empty room and as Jesse watched, it was immediately sucked up to a vent in the ceiling and disappeared.

"We still have a colony of settlers here called the Gullahs that have been here forever. They are quite talented and export their hand woven baskets to all over the world."

"Really?" Jesse took another drink of the bourbon and again savored the smoothness of the journey as it slid down his throat. Now that he had been introduced to this new blend, he thought he would change his preferred choice to this, something different. "Do they live around here?" He asked.

"They've got their own land over on the east side. This island is only twelve miles long and sometimes only two miles wide. They have owned that side for decades and have settler's rights and the families have lived there since way before we found our way over here." She raised her glass and took a hefty drink.

"I've seen in the papers that real estate is priced low." Jesse mentioned.

"It's always cheaper here since we don't have to build to keep out the cold. Of course, we have to keep out the heat."

"Hell, I'm used to the blizzards up north sometimes six months out of the year. But there's skiing and snowmobiling, and then there's the change of the seasons," he added.

Shirlee smiled. "I used to live way up north when I was younger, so I remember."

"Do you miss it?" Jesse asked, wondering.

"No, not at all." She turned her smile on him. "Are you thinking of staying here?" She asked him.

"I'm looking around." Was all he could agree to.

The women having lunch got up then and trouped by on their way out. Shirlee smiled at them. "Thank you ladies, it's nice to see you again. Should I reserve a table again next week for you?" To which they all shook their heads yes.

Jesse was not used to drinking alcohol in the afternoon and now after one he had to quit or else get loaded, which he didn't want to do. "Okay, I too need to roll," he said. "Thanks for the lovely company and I'll see you again soon." Walking out to his SUV, for some reason he had the feeling he was being watched as he got in, and inside, he lit a cigarette.

At his condo by the water, his shadow was silhouetted by the late afternoon sun as he stepped out of his vehicle. And that's when he heard three popping shots. He hit the ground. He lay on the concrete, his heart going fifty miles an hour.

What the hell? He cussed and made himself stay down. And after what seemed like an hour, but had only been five minutes, he jumped up and ran on shaky legs into his place. Inside, he called the police department again on his cell and asked for the chief.

After identifying himself to her he said, "Now, this time I know those shots are meant for me!"

"Mr. Ortega, where did it happen and when?" Juel Anderson asked.

"Jesus, here at my condo." Jesse was pissed.

"Listen, I'll have a squad over there in ten minutes." Chief Anderson said. "Stay inside!"

"Sure," Jesse clicked off his cell and swore. Was she nuts? God almighty, he wasn't going to stick around there and wait to get killed! Then taking his suitcases out of the closet threw all his clothes in and grabbed his accessory kit. Inside of five minutes he was out of there.

The .38 lay on the car seat within easy reach as he sped over the busy thorough fare back out of

Hilton Head. The highway was over a mile long and busy with tourist travel as well as locals treading their way home.

Jesse's thoughts were going a mile a minute. After all his days as a sheriff, he had dealt with a wide array of nut cases and had gotten them off the streets. But now at this late date, he couldn't think of any who might be out there, out to get him.

He cussed as he drove. What the hell is this about? Twice now he'd been in a gunman's sights. Why? He didn't know anyone down here. He stopped at a bar on the outskirts of town. God almighty, he needed to have a drink. He wasn't used to imbibing at this time of the day, but hell this was his new life and for Christ's sake it could be his last. He pulled in and parked at a place called The Snake Pit.

The first person he saw when he stepped in the dark place and climbed on a stool at the bar was Georgia, who greeted him with a smile and bent over with a kiss.

-9-

The Blue Marina was one of the up-scale places to go in Hilton Head. It was a club that catered to its many affluent residents. Some were permanent, and some who spent long week-ends or the season, depending on their wants. The docks lining the shore of the ocean were lined with yachts and sail boats of every kind and description, and with the colored lights emanating from some of their interiors, the place had a carnival feel. Dining was outside on the wharf tonight and soft classical music was furnished by a group called "The Golden Strings." The tempting aroma of grilling steaks permeated the air and mixed with the customer's perfumes. Heads turned as Elle and Hamp, the handsome couple followed the maître d' to a cozy table close to the dance floor. The last traces of the setting sun sent trailing beams of orange and violet over the crowd as it bounced over the gentle waves of the water near-by. And the hue from the setting sun was kind to the crowd by softening the lines and bulges, giving everyone an air of confidence.

"We'll have two Manhattans on the rocks, please." Hamp said to a hovering waiter and moved his chair closer to Elle. He put his arm over the back. He gazed over the room, acknowledging smiles and waves from friends and acquaintances.

Elle had been observing him and said, "Hamp, you seem to be well known in here."

"Well, my dear, this is my town."

"I can see that. Have you been here long?" She ran a hand over her perfectly fluffed red hair after a sudden breeze.

"I have for years and I've gotten to know this place well, as I've lived here and there."

"Have you been in banking long?" She asked curiously.

Hamp put an elbow on the white linen covered table. "For well over forty years."

"Well, I sure thank you for helping me set up my accounts." She smiled at the waiter then as he was back with their order. He placed the wonderful looking drinks down on their table.

They were both silent as they tasted their Manhattans. Then leaning back Elle asked, "Hamp, I know very little about you. I'm assuming you are single aren't you?"

"My dear, of course I'm free and available." He laughed then and she almost felt foolish and wondered whatever had made her ask that? She wasn't sure.

She had walked into his bank some months ago while on vacation, and inquired about prices and locations of houses for sale in the area. He had asked what she had in mind to spend and after she had told him the amount, he had seemed to be much more charming. She had teased him about that.

"Oh well," he countered, "it's not often a beautiful lady show's up on my doorstep with a purse full of money."

"Really, I would imagine it happens a lot for you!" she had said.

-10-

"Where did this happen, Mr. Ortega?" Chief Juel Anderson had asked Jesse when he had called her on his cell.

"Just as I got out of my vehicle at my condo," he answered impatiently.

"How many shots were fired?"

Jesse ran a hand over his mustache. "Another three," he answered again.

"Now I want you to stay inside and I'll be over shortly to check out the scene." He had caught her just before she hung up.

"Excuse me, chief. Just so you know I'm not there anymore."

"Why not?" She exclaimed. "Where are you then?"

Jesse looked around at the bar and found a matchbook and said, "It says here, the Snake Pit!"

"Oh for Christ sake, you think you'll be safer there? We get calls from there at least once every day." She sounded pissed.

"Yeah, well nobody's shooting at me here yet," He couldn't help saying sarcastically and added, "I got the hell away as fast as I could."

"I need you to answer some questions, Mr. Ortega, so please stay on the phone. Now I need to know, just where you were then those shots were fired. And how do you know they were aimed at you?"

"Jesus Christ, I just told you as I got out of my vehicle, I could feel the air shift as they were just inches from my head." He blew out a breath. "And wouldn't you say now the bullets were meant for me."

"Yes, Mr. Ortega, but now I would say they were meant to scare you, not kill you. You'd be dead by now otherwise!"

"Don't you think I know that chief?" Jesse flung back.

"I'd advise you to leave that bar immediately and find some out of the way place to stay for now."

"I'm considering it. I'll get back to you." And Jesse hung up. Now coming back to his barstool, he grinned at his new found friend and ordered whiskey on the rocks and a gin tonic for her. It wouldn't hurt to look at a smiling woman as he thought this dilemma through.

But after another drink and some bar snacks, Jesse got the hell out of there, after looking around. He was sure he picked out every other guy in there was carrying some form of weapon, just like him. This time no shots whirled through the air as he got in the SUV and took off after laying his .38 on the seat again. This time he found a quiet place and checked in for the night. He turned on the TV and opened a suitcase for his toothbrush.

The next morning was sunny and Jesse stretched luxuriously in the king sized bed. Jesus, he had spent the last thirty some years sleeping next to a woman, and here he was for the first time alone in one. He stared at the ceiling in the motel as his thoughts circled back to then, always feeling his soon to be ex-wife's warmth in their bed.

Oh hell, he grumbled, that time is over. And this feels wonderful! He tossed the covers off and stood up.

He had started exercising several weeks ago and now each day they became easier as he worked out. And, now as he counted the riffs his body didn't scream like it did earlier from the pain. After a shower he studied himself in the mirror over the sink as he shaved, and he liked what he saw. Some of the worry lines had disappeared from his forehead and face. And after slimming down, he was looking pretty darn good. He mumbled to himself, now if only I could enjoy this status and not get killed in the meantime!

One thing he missed was having his friends, Reed and Eddy to pal around with. He punched up three bed pillows and got comfortable and called his good buddy Reed.

"Conners," he said, "are you up?"

"Hell no, for Christ sake, it's only six o'clock, and it's a rainy morning here."

"You want me to call back?" Jesse asked.

"Nah, where the hell are you?" Reed cleared his throat.

"I'm on an island in South Carolina. It's beautiful and sunny here."

"Yeah? What the hell are you doing way down there anyway?" He could hear Reed exhale.

"I've always wanted to check out the south. But listen here's why I called. First of all, how's Eddy doing?"

"He's doing okay but still walks with a slight limp."

"Tell him I'll call soon. But Reed listen to this, some bastard is taking pot-shots at me. On two separate occasions, clean rifle shots! But, if they were meant to take me out, I'd be dead now."

"Goddammit Jesse, who the hell knows you're there?"

"No one!" Jesse remarked.

"How did it come down?" Reed wanted to know.

Jesse tossed the pillows and sat up and ran over the details. "I got the hell out of there and found a new location," he added.

"Did you call it in?" Reed asked.

"Yup. The department is run by a woman who inherited it. She didn't get too excited about it though."

"How are you going to handle this?" Reed asked.

"I've been thinking, first of all I'm going to get rid of my SUV. I might lease for now, and then do some investigating on my own."

"Yeah, I would too, but stay in touch with the department there. Call me."

Jesse clicked off his cell. He stood in the shower and let the hot water take out some of the usual aches and pains, even tried a few words to the song called "Why me, Lord", in an effort to get over the new stress of who the hell was out to get him, and why?

He drove back over the huge water parkway and back into Savannah and began to shop the car lots. First of all, he was intrigued with the convertibles. Down in this part of the country, it seemed everyone had one. Over time he'd had his share of large aristocratic black tombs or rather his ex-wife had, but hell, he wanted a change for himself. He settled on a

2014 Mercedes convertible. With the addition of a wearing a sun visor and the newest style sunglasses, he had changed his looks to that of a local. He also checked into a Hilton Hotel for now and again unpacked.

The next day he drove back over to the Beach Club condo, parked and then found a seat amongst the sun worshippers lined up next to the water and leaned back and began to watch and wait.

-11-

Jesse Ortega sat on the beach at the Hilton Head Beach Club and watched the strollers as they marched up and down the sand. Some covered from head to toe from the sun and others barely covered. In all his days he had never seen so many that went about like that. Now he might be a prude from the sticks, he just couldn't see why females exposed themselves so flagrantly. How about some mystery?   Ahh- hell, maybe he was truly from the sticks at that, he grumbled under his breath.

He had moved his sand chair around so he could see the parking lot as well, and aside from the distractions, behind his dark glasses he was busy viewing the sights. As of yet nobody, seemed to be of special interest.

After an hour in the sun, Jesse found a shaded area and stretched out in a reclining beach chair and opened a satchel of reading material he'd bought earlier. There was an assortment of thrillers he'd always planned on catching up on and now that he was retired, this was it. But, how much now would he have time for since he was still chasing killers? His own, that was!

After another hour he was still on page three in the first book, and now he was tired and hungry. Maybe he'd stop in and have a sandwich at Shirlee's Café; he was just thinking about it when out of the corner of his eye he saw a lone man seemingly strolling leisurely around the dunes. What caught his attention was the guy was wearing too many clothes for the temperature.

Jesse's interest peaked as he kept watching. The man was about fifty yards from him and Jesse could just barely make out his features. He looked to be around six feet, mid age, and wore long jeans and a long sleeved blue shirt. He stood for minutes at a time behind the tall sea oats and then moved on, further down the beach. As Jesse watched, the person of interest came back and hastily disappeared in the parking area. If his car was there it must have been way in the back as Jesse did not see him drive out. Or else he didn't!

After another thirty minutes, Jesse went to his own car and back to his new hotel, all the while watching for any vehicle that might be following him. After a shower he drove to the café. Shirlee was there today and behind the bar.

"Hey Jesse," she greeted him. "Good to see you again."

"Same here." Jesse straddled a stool. "How are things today?" He asked.

"We had another packed lunch. I'm lucky to be here right on the beach so it's convenient. Want something cold?" She asked and smiled.

"Sound's good." After a morning in the sun again, Jesse's Latin skin had turned a copper colored brown and glowed against his white teeth and graying hair.

Shirlee busied herself at the bar and coming back said, "I'm giving you a taste of some extra good bourbon called Makers Mark. Give it a try and with this one, you don't need ice, only water on the side." She smiled at him and then had to take care of a group of boisterous customers who had just clamored in.

A good ten minutes went by and Jesse savored the bourbon. Now this was good! It just seemed to melt on his tongue as it slid smoothly down his throat and when it hit his belly, instead of exploding there with a thug, it just settled over his innards peaceably, and he felt it relax his total body. And he stood there with a smile on his face when she came back to his place at the bar.

"Do you like it?" She asked.

Jesse nodded, "Now this is exceptional," he said to her.

"Would you like another?" She asked.

"Thank you but not until later, right now I need a sandwich." And she handed him a menu.

After eating a luscious Rueben, he asked for his tab. "I have some things to take care of, but I will stop in later. Thank you again for the bourbon, you certainly sold me on a good one!"

"It's one of the best," she offered. "Hurry back, every evening we have a cocktail party starting at five, then dinner from six till ten, followed by music. And guess who supplies that?" She smiled and winked.

"I'll have to stop in then," he offered.

Back in his new leased Mercedes convertible, he donned a brimmed cap and checked out the sights. He figured in this new look he was safe. And he was. Several days went by and he joined a golf club and got his game back and now really enjoyed it. He found another area to stay at and this time unpacked for good. Maybe later after he became more familiar with the place and thought he wanted to stay on, he'd think about something more permanent. And he was back on a new beach, getting his morning exercise. Although not as vigilant as before thinking, "well hell, maybe those shots were not meant for me after all!"

It was an early cloudy day with a cold wind and not a lot of strollers were braving the elements. Jesse was just into a brisk mile when he heard three brief pops rush past his head.

He hit the ground. God almighty, he yelled but his words were muffled in the sand. He laid flat for minutes. Then got up and on shaking legs ran for cover to a beach bar a couple of blocks away. He was safe, but what now?

"A shot of bourbon," he ordered and sat down at the bar. God almighty, he mumbled again under his breath and his hand shook as he raised the glass to his lips. Now for sure, he knew someone was out there gunning for him. He sat there thinking it through.

First of all, he should get out of this town and travel further down the road. But Jesus, he was just too pissed to up and run. Besides, he liked the place and most of the people in it. Sitting there awhile he decided to call Juel Anderson again, the Chief of Police, even though he didn't think she would do much.

"Where have you been Mr. Ortega, I've been worried about you?" She said.

"Really?" Well, that was a surprise. "I've been fine until today again." He told her. "I've moved around and changed cars and now I got the same three shots aimed at my head again!"

"For God's sake, do you have any new ideas?"

"Not much, but last week I did see a man looking suspicious lurking over on the Lighthouse beach."

"Did you get a good look at him?" The chief asked.

"Nope, too far away, then he disappeared." Jesse took another drink of his bourbon and lit a smoke.

"Mr. Ortega, why don't you stop in here at my office and we can carefully go over these situations."

"Okay, guess this wouldn't be good advertising for tourism if this got out!" God damn, the devil made me do it, he thought and almost laughed. Only it was so true. "I can be there in a few minutes," he agreed and finished his bourbon.

Today as he walked into the Police Department of Hilton Head Island, he was surprised to see Chief Anderson decked out in a street dress of deep pink, exposing her tanned bare arms, low neckline and above the knee hemline.

"Excuse me, I just got back from a meeting of our political board and haven't had time to change into my official suit," she explained as she saw his eyes wonder over her.

"Ahh-, you do justice to this look too." Jesse offered with a grin.

"Come on in and take a seat. Refresh my memory, now when was the first time this happened?" She asked and they went over each time minute by minute.

"Mr. Ortega, I will have my men keep their eyes open for someone loitering around the beaches fitting your description. Why don't you join a health club and stay off them."

"A good idea," he said. And then grinning he asked, "Chief why don't you join me for dinner this evening?"

She looked at him in surprise and then smiled. "Well, maybe I could do that."

"Okay, do you want to meet me somewhere?" Jesse asked.

"I can, how about downtown at the Fisherman's Wharf. It's right on the water in the Cove."

"What time?" Jesse wanted to know. "I need to stop at my hotel."

"An hour, I'll need that to finish up here. And you can call me Juel."

At his hotel it took him thirty minutes to get ready and he looked and smelled like a million bucks as he drove back downtown and to the restaurant.

Things were moving along nicely for them over dinner and wine until Juel said "Yesterday, a young girl was found dead in the dunes over by that condo where you first stayed." She raised her martini glass.

-12-

The evening with Elle and Hampton moved along smoothly as they enjoyed a night out at the Blue Marina in Hilton Head. She felt more relaxed now after a Manhattan as they nibbled on their shrimp cocktails and crackers, and the eerie happenings at her home earlier were fading fast. Also doubt invaded her recollection of the scary incident; like the dispatcher at police department had said, it all could have been attributed to the storms in the region.

"Now that you've had time in your new home, is it everything you were looking for?" he asked her.

"Mostly Hamp and yes I'm pretty sold on the place." She hadn't mentioned the incident earlier to him. "I love living by the ocean and the ever rolling waves have a lulling effect for me. Do you live on the water as well?" She asked.

Hamp smiled. "Yes, on a plantation."

"Really?"   Elle smiled. "You have the whole plantation?" She asked.

"But it's small," He murmured.

"Well, what do you call small? Are you talking about a gated community of homes that is called a plantation?"

"No, not exactly, I'm the only resident." He didn't speak with a lot of enthusiasm and she wondered why. Then, seemingly to cover a pause in their conversation he said, "Why don't you let me order for you?"

Elle agreed but added, "And I like most everything except things that are red."

Hamp looked at her and laughed, "You mean red meat, red sauce and red liquor?"

Elle smiled. "Yes, that about covers it."

"Well, that leaves only fish and seafood." He murmured and studied the menu.

As the waiter came over and took the order, Elle looked around the restaurant at the colorful crowd. She saw a lot of couples and groups of people all seemingly having a good time. And for a moment she felt somewhat jealous of their apparent comradely time.

Elle hadn't lived in Hilton Head more than a few months and hadn't formed many friendships yet. Now as they were waiting for their dinner, Hamp said to her, "I've got a place I want to take you to called Shirlee's. Have you been there yet?"

"No, not as yet, Hamp. I just haven't taken the time to go out much."

"Well, you're in for a treat. It's just a few doors down." He smiled at her and tipped his cocktail glass to hers.

"Okay, I love to meet new people. Not that I can't do it by myself, of course." Elle added.

Then they were served the seafood delicacies Hamp had ordered. There was a crab Louie salad, lobster linguini with charred asparagus, and crusty bread fresh from the oven accompanied by a lovely ice cold chardonnay.

The music was soft and relaxing and made conversation easy. As they paused in their eating and sipped their wine, Hamp asked, "Elle, what are you planning on keeping busy with here in Hilton Head?"

Elle smiled. "I haven't decided yet. But something fun, of course." She hadn't told anyone that she was a pretty well-known journalist yet.

"Well, you'll let me enjoy those times with you too then?" Hamp added.

Elle was feeling good by now and agreed. He took another long sip of the wine.

"Do you have family here in Hilton Head?" She asked next.

"No," he answered.

"Do you have any children?"

He shook his head, and suddenly irritated, blurted out, "My dear, is this an inquisition?" And then, laughed slightly to cover his embarrassment when he realized how he had sounded.

Elle looked at him and frowned, suddenly realizing she'd touched on a sensitive subject. She forked another piece of lobster meat in her mouth and wondered what that was all about.

"Inquisition, hardly!" She said and couldn't help but add, "Hamp, you're a free agent just as I am. Now, if I want to find out what a person is really like, I hire it done."

There, she sat back and grinned inwardly.

Hamp was quiet for a while as they finished their dinner. After paying the check he took her arm as they left the restaurant and waited for the valet to bring his car around.

Driving just a few businesses down the beach, he again gave his car to a valet and they stepped into Shirlee's Café. Here the place was absolutely rocking the rafters in the oldies song called "Sweet Caroline," with Shirlee at the grand piano. They stood in the middle of the room as not a single chair or stool was available. Hamp elbowed his way to the bar and got them each a Baileys and found a corner of the bar for their drinks.

Elle tapped her toe as she hummed to the song. Being brought up with music in the house by her mother and brothers, she was totally savvy. Music made her joyful most of the time, but then again, it could bring her to her knees in misery if she wasn't careful. Tonight, however she was intent on that not happening.

After another group of high-spirited songs were finished, Shirlee came over to them.

"Good evening, thank you for coming." She exclaimed and smiled.

"Hello Shirlee," Hamp said, "I can see you've got a good thing going."

"Thank you." She smiled at Elle and reached for her hand. "My name is Shirlee," she said and Hamp stepped in and said, "And this is Elle Moore, a new resident of our fair city." The ladies shook and being true to their sex quickly checked each other's attire.

"Lovely place," Elle returned her smile, "and I bet you have great lunches as well."

"And we'd love to stop in," He added.

For a moment, Elle felt irritated at his assumption that they were a couple and would have another date. In the last decade being a "free agent" she had gotten along just fine!

-13-

Jesse and Police Chief Juel Anderson were at a downtown Hilton Head restaurant when she told him that a young girl had been found dead the day before at The Beach Club.

Jesse set his water glass down hard on their table. "You mean on that same beach, at the place where I was first staying at?"

The chief nodded. "She was found in the dunes on the beach."

"Oh Jesus," Jesse exclaimed. He swiped a hand over his mustache. It took a few minutes for him to continue and then he asked, "Did you still have someone over there on a stake out?"

Chief Anderson took a swallow of her martini and shook her head sadly. "No, I had pulled the guys off that area and had them over at the second place, where those rifle shots were fired at you again."

Jesse's voice sounded hoarse as he asked, "How old was she?"

Chief Anderson grimaced, "She was only seventeen, and I had the sad task of informing her family."

"Oh man, I sure know how that feels." After a few moments Jesse wanted to know, "Was she out by herself on the beach?"

"She was a runner. Listen to this; she was training to compete in the next Olympics. Her family said she always ran several hours before a light dinner. And when it had gotten dark and after nine o'clock that night, and she hadn't come back, they called us. We found her several hours later."

"Had she been raped?" Jesse asked sadly.

"Yes." Chief Juel's face paled. "And her neck had been broken. The medical examiner said that she apparently put up a huge fight as she had a lot bruising all over her body."

"Man, oh man!" Jesse whispered again hoarsely, and swiped a hand over his mustache then, trying hard to regain his composure, "Have you got anybody that looks suspicious?" he wanted to know.

"Not one so far." Chief Juel answered.

Jesse stroked his chin. "Could it have been a serial killer?" He asked curiously.

"Yes, but this is a first here in Hilton Head since the 70's. Then we had one case similar to this. A young girl too and my dad was the chief then and he never found the killer."

"Did you get any prints of this one?" Jesse asked. His beer sat untouched in front of him.

"We got a partial off her wrist watch band but it could be her own. I've got a call in to the BCA, the National Bureau of Criminal Investigations. They'll run the information I sent, with known sex offenders. So I should hear from them in the morning."

"If it is a serial killer, you know 90 percent are men in their twenties or thirties, and usually are loners," Jesse went on to say. "Have you picked up any vagrants lately?"

"Oh sure, but I didn't find any in the files that looked good for it," Chief Juel said and went on, "I know the habits start at a young age like bed wetting after the age of twelve, also are killers of defenseless small animals after making them suffer. God, it makes me sick to think we may have such a monster right here in our midst!"

Jesse asked, "Chief, have you had any strange fires in the area, or, had any suspicious deaths?"

"You know, I sat up late into the night last night, and went over every single case that has crossed my desk in the five years I've been in office. Nothing jumped out that made me wonder." She blew out a breath.

Now Jesse could see the fine lines around her eyes and hear the exhaustion in her voice. The neckline of her rose colored dress fell lower on her chest as she shrugged her shoulders up and down to relieve the tension in them.

And Jesse felt drawn to the lovely view and said, "Listen chief, let me help you. I'm pretty good at this and sometimes a fresh eye will see something that can be easily overlooked."

Chief Juel looked at him and shook her head. "Thanks Jesse, but I can't do that without permission from our city council, and we're over extended already they say."

"Yeah, I know the drill." Jesse mumbled.

"Do you mind if we order, I've got to say I haven't eaten much today. And it feels wonderful to sit and relax, but when we finish I've got to hurry back to the office." They were silent as they studied the menu. And after both decided on a steak and a salad they caught the waiter and ordered.

"Can I bring you another martini," he asked the chief and she smiled and said, "No thanks, not tonight."

They said good night a short time later and as they waited for their cars, Jesse asked, "Chief, okay if I call you later on and see how things are going?"

"Of course, but stay off the beaches now, promise?" She smiled at him as she got in the cruiser, and didn't hurry to adjust the hemline of her dress as it slid up to show well rounded thighs. She tossed her purse on the passenger seat and closed the door.

Jesse liked what he saw as he drove out into the street too, but he was heart sick. At first, he had been pissed to have been the intended focus for this nut case. And now, to find out a poor defenseless girl had been raped and then murdered. Could it have been by the same character?   He thought again of that suspicious looking stranger he had seen on the beach several nights before. God almighty, he had to find the bastard!

But how the hell had this predator found him, again here at the Grand Hotel? Christ, this was the third place he'd checked into. Miles in between each one, and now he even had been driving a different set of wheels.

After a time, it finally occurred to him. Yeah well dummy, there's only one way, he mumbled. The fucker has been following me because he's slipped a tracking devise on my vehicles!

It was going on nine o'clock and the sunset was at its peak over the water, Jesse saw as he drove into the underground parking garage at the hotel. He took the elevator up to his fourth floor suite and then sank down in a chair and put his feet up on the ottoman. He didn't have a balcony at this place but he could open the big screened window for the breeze, and see the ocean that was only a few yards from the building.

He dropped his head on the back of the chair and took a deep breath. Jesus, he felt responsible for the young girl's death. Should he go and see her family and try to explain? He suspected that when the nutcase hadn't found him to take some more pot shots at, the fucker took his revenge and misplaced anger out on this poor innocent girl. Serial killers and murderers had similar cunning traits. And somehow, this person had tricked the young girl and although she was a runner and in good physical health, he had to have gotten close enough to disable her, making it impossible for her to get away.

Jesse swore. Was there no way he could get away from all this bullshit? Here he was right back in the middle of it again! But why was this asshole after him in the first place? And what the hell was behind it?

-14-

Elle glanced over at Hamp as he drove her home. After that swaggering remark, his arrogant assumption had caused her to see a domineering streak in him. Although the man was handsomely dressed and had impeccable manners, there was just something about him that irritated her. At her house, he jumped out of the car and held the door for her.

"Now my dear, you are going to invite me in for a nightcap, aren't you?" he asked as they went up to her door.

"I'm sorry, Hamp, tonight is not good," Elle murmured, "I need to get eight hours or else I'm not good at what I do."

"Well, that sounds mysterious Elle. What do you do?"

"Oh, I just do some writing." She smiled.

"Well hell, what did you do before?"

"Before what?" She remembered his obvious, sudden interest when she had told him what she would pay for a home here on the island. She laughed now. "Don't you just really want to know how I came to be so rich?"

"Well, you got me there Elle. How did you?" Hamp reached out a hand, as she took her house keys out of her purse, but turning away from him she unlocked the double door herself.

"I just got lucky," she said and then leaned over and kissed his cheek.

"Thank you Hamp, I had a lovely time. The Blue Marina is indeed a great supper club."

"Can we get together again later in the week?" He asked.

"Call me and we'll see." And she firmly closed the door and clicked the locks. She laid her wrap and purse down on a table in the vestibule, and walked through her house to the kitchen. On the way she stopped at the liquor cabinet in the library and poured herself a brandy and took it back to the kitchen counter and sat.

There was so much she had to take time and think through. First of all, Hamp hadn't turned out to be that "knight in shining armor" as she had previously thought when they had talked on the phone. The vibes she'd felt coming from him tonight were all wrong. Was it just his assuming attitude that irritated her? Usually she was pretty good at reading people, and it wouldn't be the first time that some man had tried to take over her life, and, her finances.

The second thing that was troubling her was the paintings that were still in the house on her wall. At the first several showings of the house, the realtor had said the art would be picked up and taken out. Yet at the closing sale the paintings were still there. The sale was handled by an attorney representing the owners who were traveling abroad, and they didn't know anything about the artwork. So, according to her own attorney, after not getting any response to a posting in a newspaper, the art came with the sale of the house and now, she was the owner.

Strange, Elle murmured. She took the brandy with her and went into the living room. She turned on all the lamps, and then went to stand in front of the art covered wall.

There were a total of fourteen paintings, both large and small. And being somewhat of a connoisseur of art, these all looked to be of professional quality. She searched again for the artists name or initials on the front and back of each and studied each one carefully. There was nothing! But then after another thorough examination again, she did find a small brush stroke of red in the lower right corner of each one that somewhat resembled a bird in flight. So carefully hidden that unless you were studying each one you wouldn't notice them.

By now, Elle had finished the brandy and she stood back and thought about the situation. First of all, she'd contact a friend who dealt in art in Savannah, and see what he thought about the situation and go from there.

The next few days flew by as she spent time in her office on her computer finishing up a story she had been working on for publication. Elle Moore was a writer, for a well-known newspaper and wrote under another name. She had won several awards for articles, after going out in the field to investigate the subject. She had been around the world on assignments and had one coming up that might prove to be another winner. But she had several more days yet to relax. However, today she closed down her laptop after several early morning hours. She showered, dressed and got in her car and went out to spend the day at a spa she had found that catered to the whole woman. She had a standing weekly appointment for a massage, a facial and waxing, hair care, and a mani-pedi. She always left feeling energized as her red hair gleamed and her skin was smooth and glowing.

She liked to spend the rest of the day shopping, and then have a leisurely cocktail and an early supper. She went out to Shirlee's Cafe again and walked in out of the hot southern sunshine to the cool ambience of the place. Shirlee was behind the bar and greeted her with a welcoming smile.

"I see you're at work." Elle smiled at her new acquaintance. Hamp had introduced them several days before.

Shirlee nodded. "I always send my bartender out to take a break at this time of the day. We always have a busy lunch business so she needs to eat and regroup."

"I bet she appreciates that." Elle sat on a bar stool and laid her purse on the bar.

"Have you ever tried a champagne cocktail?" Shirlee asked her. "If not I'll make us each one." And a few minutes later they each took their first sip of the refreshing cool concoction.

Elle had looked around the room on her way in. The bar was ebony stained, rectangular in shape with stools that had red leather seats. Tall tables and red covered stools took up one side of the bar. A big baby grand piano was located so it could be seen from both sides of the room, and the dining room on the other side was separated by glossy trees and plants. There the tables had white linen tablecloths, red napkins and a single fresh red rose centerpiece on each one. Sparkling wine glasses stood ready and inviting on each one as well. The walls were white brick and had lovely large oil paintings with red as their theme colors. Soft music came from speakers located around the room.

"I love your place Shirlee," Elle remarked. "Did you design it yourself?"

Shirlee laughed. "I did. When I bought this, it was just a rundown saloon that had been built years ago. So I had it torn down and drew up the new plans."

"Well, you did a good job."

"What about you Elle, have you been here in Hilton Head long?" Shirlee smiled at Elle. "We didn't get a chance to talk the other night when you came in."

"I know, I'm sorry, I've been here six months now." Elle picked the hazelnut from at her cocktail and popped it into her mouth.

And Shirlee greeted a new customer and said, "Hello, Jesse good to see you, can I bring you some of that fine Kentucky bourbon I introduced you to?"

-15-

Jesse hit the sack but couldn't get to sleep. Back in Birch, the majority of the time he slept from exhaustion most nights and automatically woke every morning at six a.m. and here, no matter how late he stayed up, his eyes still sprang open at early dawn. But that was okay for today, as he planned his own stake out.

After breakfast in the coffee shop in the hotel, he went back to his room and got ready to go back down to the beach where he had seen that overdressed man several days ago, and who had mysteriously disappeared. Maybe today the guy would show up again. At the beach, he rented a beach chair from an outdoor vender, slathered on sun tan lotion and settled in. He'd added a western style straw hat to his get up and behind his dark glasses now as he sat, his glance roamed from left to right as he studied each and every person. The place was busy with runners, strollers and numerous individuals and groups who had spread towels or opened a beach chair and gathered to visit.

Jesse resembled a local with his already dark tan, and with his Latin heritage he might have been a traveler from the Southwest here on holiday. He sat looking totally relaxed, and engrossed in his book, but that was not the case. There looked to be at least a hundred people spread out on the sand. And it was uncanny how quiet it was. Just a strain of music would drift over once in a while from a boom box and then there might be an occasional shriek, from time to time as someone tested the water. Other than that, the voices from the large arena of populace were softened by the lulling waves.

Jesse's cell phone rang just then. When he heard his wife's voice he immediately thought it might be an emergency. Jesse Junior, their twenty four year old son, lived in Minneapolis and was an electrical engineer for a national company. He was healthy, and encouraged his parents to get along, even if they were not together.

The minute her grating voice came over the line, Jesse cringed in irritation.

"Why are you calling me, is Junior okay?" He asked in a low voice.

"He's fine Jesse, but I want you to come back. I don't like being alone in this big house." She exclaimed with the same whining edge that always got him.

"Well, why don't you sell it then and get something smaller," He remarked.

"No Jesse, I want you to come back. You belong here in Birch."

He shook his head exclaiming, "No, not anymore. It's over!" And he didn't want to tell her he was happy in this new life, or she might decide to withdraw the claim just out of spite.

"Jesse, I don't want a divorce after all. Come back and we'll talk to the minister. He can help us."

"For Christ sake, I won't allow even him into my business. Forget it and get real. Don't call me again unless the kid gets sick or hurt." And he hung up.

God almighty, he mumbled under his breath. That woman is never satisfied. He downed a bottle of water and it took him some time before he could settle in again to waiting and watching.

As yet, he hadn't seen anyone walking the beach or sunning themselves that looked to be of interest. But it didn't mean the perpetrator wasn't around. He could be just lying low for now too, and watching for Jesse to stroll by on a walk. He could also be one of the many single individuals hidden behind their glasses and assorted books and papers, or one, only pretending to be taking a nap. Jesse hadn't dared take his eyes off the scene for fear he might miss something, but he was getting tired. When he checked his watch he saw he had been there in the sun for hours and even after opening the chair to the lounge position and turning over on his stomach and resting his chin on his hands, he was tired.

Well hell, he mumbled, this is it. If the fucker is out here somewhere, just let him try to take some shots at me today. But as he walked off the beach and over the dunes he had to force himself not to run like hell. He remembered too, he'd parked the Mercedes a block away in another hotel's lot and now he wished it wasn't so damn far away. Back at his hotel he took a much needed nap.

It was going on five when he awoke to the sound of his cell ringing. When he picked it up, Reed Conners was on the line.

"Hey buddy," Reed said and asked, "What's going on down there on the island now?"

"A hell of a lot," Jesse commented. "Since we talked the other day, now I find out, a young girl was found raped and dead on that very same beach where I was first shot at."

"For Christ sake, Jesse, why don't you get the hell out of there before it's too late?" Reed said hurriedly.

"It's not that easy. I've moved two more times and changed my vehicle and the fucker still found me and took another three shots at me. It finally dawned on me he has been following me around because he'd put a tracker on my wheels.

"Goddamn Jesse, someone wants you out of that town."

"I got the message, but why? I don't know a fucking soul here." Jesse blew out a breath as he sat on the edge of the bed. He pulled the pillows together and leaned back on them.

"Is that police chief more cooperative now?" Reed asked.

"Oh yeah, she took me serious after that poor young girl was killed." Jesse stood up and went to the small refrigerator in the desk for a bottle of water.

"Listen pal," Reed went on to say. "I've got another reason for calling. Your wife wants me to drop the divorce. Said she's changed her mind and wants you back."

"Oh goddamn, no way!" Jesse exclaimed. "Remind her that we both signed papers stating just that, amongst other things."

"Okay Jesse, I just wanted to make sure you were still on for it. I'll call her back and let her know the divorce is still going forward."

"Thanks. And remind her if she does go with some other lawyer, she pays for it as it is stated in those papers."

"I'm on it, Jesse. Now to get back to the scene there, are you carrying?"

"Absolutely, after that first time those shots just missed my head." Jesse went to stand by the large window and watched the waves come in from out on the ocean.

"I just had a thought, have you checked the gun laws there, about tourists carrying?" Reed wanted to know.

"Hell no." Jesse admitted.

"Goddamn, buddy, check with the state licensing board on gun permits for non-residents. Better to be safe than sorry in the end." Reed added.

"Christ, you're right. Thanks for reminding me, I should have remembered that I'm not the law anymore, here either."

"It's just a reminder to be on the safe side, Jesse. Here's another thought. I think it would be wise to trade in the SUV and get something else to drive."

"I ended up trading off the SUV already and I'm leasing a convertible which is common around here. Then, I realized I'd been made and that I was being followed. I'm getting rid of this one too."

"Good you're on it. Now be careful!"

"Yeah, thanks pal." Jesse reassured Reed and they clicked off their cells.

He shaved and showered, and used his new cologne the sales girl at Nordstrom had sold him because she said "every man should use a fragrance." Leaving the convertible at the hotel, this late afternoon he traveled by taxi and when he walked into Shirlee's Café, the first person he saw was this gorgeous redhead sitting by herself at the bar. Suddenly his world looked a hell of a lot brighter.

Not to be too obvious about wanting to meet her, he took a bar stool several down from hers. After the bartender took his order he looked over and grinned, then asked, "Are you a resident of this fair city?"

She smiled at him, "I wasn't until lately then I decided to become one."

Jesse stood up and moved closer. He held out his hand. "Names Jesse Ortega and I'm undecided."

"Really? I can't understand why," and added, "My name is Elle Moore." Her hand felt small and cool in his as they shook.

And he wanted to hang on to it and maybe even kiss it. What the hell, he had never been a romantic, but for some reason all of a sudden now, he felt like he was. And, he actually felt tongue tied as he searched for something intelligent to say, then settled on, "You're staying on then?" Shirlee, the bartender brought his bourbon over. He remained standing.

"I am," Elle replied. "I purchased a house here and love it."

And, if he could have read her thoughts, maybe her look was casual but her thoughts were anything but.

-16-

When Jesse had strolled into Shirlee's café and stood at the bar, the first person he saw was Elle Moore. She smiled at him and all through their conversation so far, he had a hard time concentrating.

He smoothed a hand over his mustache. Damn, but all these women here in the south were so friendly and he wasn't used to all this seemingly open "come on" attitudes they portrayed. But maybe he was reading them all wrong. He took a hefty drink of his bourbon. Well hell, he liked it. He sure as hell hadn't gotten any of this attention back in Birch. There he was just a middle aged, overworked, overweight sheriff who worked his ass off. Who never even got laid at home anymore!

Oh man, he wondered to himself. How long would I have stayed locked in that scene and not bolted.

His attention was brought back to the scene in the café, as Elle began to tell about her new home by the water. "And I'm planning on having a get acquainted party soon and inviting friends I've met so far.

The sheriff in Jesse immediately brought out a cautionary comment. "I'd be careful about that Elle; it's easy to lose control over the guest list."

"I know, but none of my acquaintances seem unsavory." Elle finger combed her red tresses as she talked.

"But you don't know that," Jesse warned.

Shirlee had stood listening to their exchange. "Girlfriend," she smiled, "here's what you can do. Invite Jesse, he looks able and he can keep an eye out for any and all of those who do look sleazy."

"Really?" Elle smiled sweetly and looking him over remarked, "Hmm-, maybe."

He had never mentioned to Shirlee or Elle that he was a retired sheriff.

Several hours passed as the new friends talked of things happening in Hilton Head and also of tentative plans of meeting again in a few days. Jesse had wanted to ask Elle out on a date, but didn't have the time when she suddenly stood to leave.

Early the next day, he got in the convertible and after driving around for an hour to make sure he was not being followed, Jesse went to the car dealership and traded it for a nondescript white Buick. Now, this one should not attract any attention, as every other car here is white, he mumbled. On the way back to his hotel he stopped at The Diner for breakfast, the place he'd found on his first day into the town, which was just several weeks ago. He'd grown to like Hilton Head by now, and if he could figure out who the hell was trying to scare him away, he could look around for a place to settle in for a while.

As he was being shown to a table, he passed by Police Chief Juel Anderson who was sitting by herself. She was the only person who knew of his former occupation and he had felt they had a lot in common.

"Please join me," she invited.

Jesse stopped abruptly. "Well, it happens I am alone." He took the chair opposite her thinking maybe today he'd have a chance to get to know her better.

"I just ordered some eggs and grits," she said and handed him a menu. "But there's a full pot of coffee here to start with. Help yourself."

Chief Juel looked good in full uniform today wearing a navy blue jacket and skirt with a white shirt underneath. Dainty silver hoops adorned her ears and set off her blonde hair. Jesse remembered he had checked her hand for rings before and he still didn't see any on her fingers. But of course that didn't mean she wasn't attached. But she was hot!

His attention was brought back when she asked, "Mr. Ortega, I haven't heard anything from you, so that must mean you haven't been targeted again and shot at, is that right?" She looked him over, raising a perfectly shaped eyebrow.

"Now, I could take that two different ways Chief, meaning, I could be dead by now so you couldn't, or that nothing has happened since the other day." Jesse remarked dryly and rolled his shoulders. Then busied himself pouring cream in his coffee and stirring.

"Nothing new then, no new gun happy person out there, taking shots at you?" She asked.

"Nope, good so far, Chief."

"Mr. Ortega, you haven't been out there on your own, have you?" She wanted to know. "I've warned you, not to try to do this."

"Call me Jesse, please. And no, of course I'm not out there doing your job for you, foolishly putting myself in jeopardy!"

"Good, you'll let us do our work then." And she smiled at him putting emphasis on the word "our".

"Just out of curiosity, chief," Jesse asked, "have you anyone in mind who looks good, who might be my gun touting stalker?"

Chief Juel answered dryly, "Mr. Ortega, first off, right now we are working day and night trying to arrest the scum who murdered that innocent little teenager before we have another death on our hands!"

Jesse nodded and said, "I understand completely!" But couldn't keep a little sarcasm out of his voice as he added, "good to know my safety is not lost in your duties too!"

Just then, a sweet young waitress came by with an order. Setting the food down for the Chief exclaimed, "Sorry, I couldn't get back sooner, but I promise to get your order right in, so it shouldn't take more than a few minutes for the kitchen to get it ready for you."

"That's okay, I'm being delightfully entertained," Jesse laughed dryly. "And I'm in no hurry."   He watched then as Chief Juel slid her eggs over her grits, seasoned them and began to eat heartily.

When his order of scrambled eggs and toast came a few minutes later he piled his eggs on top of his toast and then sprinkled some Tabasco on it.

After finishing their breakfast and another quick cup of coffee, the chief stood up and gathered her blue shoulder bag. "Thank you for your company, Jesse," she said all business like.

"And, for yours as well." He stood as she left, and then shook his head at her apparent aloofness again today. He had thought they had a common interest as he had formerly been in the same business, but she wasn't about to let him into her world.

Well hell, he commented, then sat back down at the table and took up the local paper. After glancing through it, he saw there was not any new information on the murder of that girl found on the beach at his first hotel. He'd seen the day before that there had been an article releasing the victim's name, and a bio of this young girl's accomplishments so far in her life. Being a parent himself, and also being a sheriff and having been a bearer of such news to other parents, he knew this had to be one of the most painful things for her family to go through. He swallowed hard over the coffee as he drank the last drop. He paid his bill and got in his new white Buick to leave The Diner, still dwelling on the sadness for the family and forgetting to carefully, check over his surroundings. And he hadn't noticed as a man hid behind his newspaper in a somewhat dusty black vehicle parked a couple cars from his, or that, minutes later he was being followed by that same sedan.

-17-

Several days went by and Jesse was busy with his daily walks and sleuthing, then with just taking it easy. He had found another beach to go to and so far had not been shot at. He'd found parking at a busy golf course, and then walking a block over to a small hidden beach where it was not easily found by the public. He kept his gun at his side at all times, and still changed his attire and look daily. Today he wore a visor and aviator sun glasses. He carried his own sand chair and settled down next to a clump of sea oats. He had grown used to keeping an eye on the people around him and the walkers who paraded up and down the hardened sand next to the water.

Lately, he'd spent the evenings by himself generally giving him time to mull over again why someone could be shooting at him. Not trying to kill him, he knew by now, just giving him a message, apparently to leave town. He patiently rethought over the cases that had been his over the years as sheriff. There had been numerous ones where he'd had to put someone away in jail or prison. Some shoot outs and several times he'd had to protect his deputies and himself by killing a man. That hadn't happened often and when it had, he'd prayed for forgiveness for taking a life. Of course, that was only between him and his God.

Today, he sat with a book in his hand as he thought over his former plan. Did he really want to stay here in Hilton Head? Why the hell didn't he just get in his car and move on! He had to think about that for a while, and, then came to the conclusion that he'd already met some great people and had begun to feel at home here. Granted they were all females, and he had to smile at that. Well hell.

After several hours he packed up and found his car, but on the way back to his hotel, he stopped at a golf course and went into the pro shop. He had decided to widen his daily activities and brush-up on his golfing. And after renting clubs and a bag, and buying shoes and a shirt, he was down a few hundred bucks. Next he launched a bucket of balls. It felt good to hit the hell out of one and see it almost disappear in the distance. Pumped now, he stopped back at the pro shop and asked if there were any groups of golfers that needed another man and was told there was and to show up the next morning at 10 am, to meet the others. And after a good night's rest, he showered and slipped on the new shirt and was off.

"Good morning," he said again to the guy in the pro shop. "Are the rest of the guys here?" He asked wheeling his rented bag of clubs inside with him.

The golf pro nodded toward a group of three guys standing off to the side. "Over there," he said. And Jesse went over and held out his hand.

"Jesse Ortega," he said and each man shook his hand and told him their name. Then he grinned. "It's been years, but I hope I don't put all of you to shame right off." He joked.

"That's okay, we need the practice," a guy in orange pants offered.

The one who looked to be a hundred years old offered. "I just got off the plane from Texas and thought I'd limber up a bit."

Jesse almost laughed out loud understanding what he'd just gotten himself into. "Well hell," he said to his new found friends. "Let's hit the course and start the game!" And like kindergarten kids, they all followed him out the door to the first tee.

It wasn't long before Jesse felt like the pro as he patiently explained and showed them how to do this or that. At the finish of the ninth hole, he just had to take a break.

"Will you come by tomorrow so we can do this again?" The guy in the orange pants wanted to know. And not wanting to disappoint him, Jesse said, "maybe, but if I'm not here at 10, start without me." Actually by now, after hours on the golf course and already after lunch, Jesse just needed a drink. He'd purposely stayed away from Shirlee's Café, just in case the stalker would follow and cause some trouble in there and hurt innocent people. Now he parked the white Buick in an adjoining lot.

"Hello handsome," Shirlee called out to him as he came in the door. "You haven't been in for days now Jesse, are you okay?" She was sitting at her baby grand piano off to the side of the room.

"I'm fine, just been brushing up on my golf." He ordered some of that Kentucky blend she had suggested earlier, from the bartender. And after she had it ready, he picked up his glass and went to stand by Shirlee.

"I've been learning some new numbers for my guests tonight," she said as she ran her nimble fingers over some of notes. "Do you know this one?" she asked, then played and hummed a familiar Barbara Streisand classic.

"One of my favorites." Jesse grinned and pulled a stool over and sat. "I have that CD in my things. One of her love songs from the 80's I remember." As he looked at Shirlee, his male hormones jumped into gear and he wondered again if she was single or in a relationship. And throwing caution to the wind asked, "Okay, you can tell me to go to hell, but I'd like to know, are you unattached?" He grinned.

Shirlee smiled. "I'm single and unattached, but I have many friends."

Catching the politeness in her voice, he realized she was being diplomatic in her answer.

And to add lightness to what might have been uncomfortable for her said, "Damn, all the good ones are taken!"

She laughed then and said, "Jesse, I try not to get involved with my customers. But there are exceptions."

Well, not one to let this one go, he returned with, "good to know."

After several drinks of that smooth Kentucky blend, Jesse realized it had taken the kinks out of his sore back and now he needed to get some sleep. But after leaving Shirlee's Café and a stop to shower at his hotel, and wide awake now, he went out again to check out another new place called The Blue Marina. He smiled to himself as he parked and walked in. Back in Birch he couldn't have done this, as it would have started talk, but here and now, things had changed. He was a free agent, and free to check out all these "watering holes" if and when he pleased.

As he stepped in the foyer of The Blue Marina, he saw it was an upscale restaurant with white linen covering black skirted round tables, with individual table lamps. Waiters and wine sommeliers hovered in the room that was buzzing with customers. A handsome young man sat on a stage in a corner of the room entertaining, and at this minute he held the crowd in breathless suspension as he poured out his rendition of the classic called Rhapsody on his acoustical guitar. Jesse stopped mesmerized, to watch and listen to this man's music. Then as he stepped to the bar, he saw a familiar face.

"Hello Elle," he said and saw that apparently she was alone.

"Jesse," she said, "this is a surprise."

"It is. I've never been here before, but wanted to check it out." Then turning and looking back at the entertainer, commented, "beautiful! Did you hear that guitar?"

"Yes, the man is a genius. His name is Jeffrey and he is from New York and a friend of Shirlee's. He's also a cousin of hers."

"God almighty, just to be able to play like that," Jesse shook his head. "Mind if I join you Elle." Just then a bartender came over.

"What can I bring you," she asked.

"A Kentucky blended bourbon please." He took the stool next to Elle and grinned. "You're looking lovely tonight," he said, looking her up and down.

"Oh, these old things," she laughed and tossed her red head. Tonight she was wearing a little white strapless dress and her jewelry was silver.

"Can I get you another cocktail?" Jesse asked seeing her Manhattan was low.

"Just one. Then I have to go."

"Okay, may I ask where?"

"No, but I'd love to stay here awhile with you, Jesse. When I met you at Shirlee's last week, to me, you seemed like a mystery man. Is that so, are you?" She smiled at him.

"No, there's no mystery about me. What do you want to know?" Her refill came and another for him.

"Well, you're so in shape. I'd guess you own one of those boats that are outside here."

"Elle, you guessed wrong," He laughed. "I don't own one of those. But tell me about you, I know you bought a house on the water.'

She smiled. "Yes, and I love most things about it. It came with a lot of furniture so I've sorted out the things I want, and gotten rid of the rest."

"Is it around here?" Jesse asked.

"Yes, it's just a few blocks from here." After she finished the last of her cocktail, Elle stood up, "Jesse, come on and I'll show you."

"Well, this is great." Jesse laughed as they walked out of the place and asked, "Should I follow you in my car?"

"Yes," and she hurried over to a black BMW. In minutes they sped through the streets, and into a locked area, and then turned in to a cobble stone drive and up to a blazing white stucco rambler. The landscape was green and clipped, and cactus and succulents adorned the grounds around palm trees. It was breathtaking to Jesse.

"Follow me," Elle said as they walked together after leaving their cars. "You've got to see what I see every night," and she led him around to the back side of the house to a patio filled with lovely stuffed outdoor furniture that faced the Atlantic. By now it was pitch black outside, with just a sliver of the moon showing. But the sky over the black water was lit like a Christmas tree with thousands of stars blazing across the horizon. They both stood silently in awe.

Caught up in the moment, Elle turned into Jesse's arms and he kissed her. At first she hesitated, and then he could feel her lips soften. He slowly kissed her forehead, the tip of her nose, then came back to her lips and now they were waiting for him. He tightened his arms around her and she leaned into him.

"God almighty, you feel good Elle," he whispered in her hair. And soon their kisses became hotter and their breath shorter. Then he took her hand and led her to a one of the couches on the patio. This was it, and although Jesse desperately wanted the comfort of sex, for a minute he almost lost his nerve. It had been years being married to one woman, and he had almost been true blue, but now he suddenly wondered if things had changed out on the dating scene.

But he needn't have worried, because in seconds, Elle had slipped out of her dress and stood before him in only her bikini underwear and high heels.

"Let me help you, Jesse," she whispered and unbuttoned his shirt and tossed it away. Then unzipped his slacks and began to run her hands over his body.

Jesse groaned and helped her with his own clothes, and they both lay down on the couch. He began kissing her breasts, and moved down over her belly feathering her with gentle little kisses, and then he bent further down lifting her legs and found her vulnerable spot.

"Oh my God," Elle whispered hoarsely. Then shuddered suddenly and Jesse raised himself and entered her, then lost himself in the most glorious climax he'd ever had.

And minutes later they lay together in the night, still entwined in lust as their breath finally slowed down.

"Are you okay?" Jesse finally managed to ask her.

She sat up and smiled then said, "Ortega, you are a terror in bed." She finger combed her hair and went on, "I wanted to show you my house, so come." And then without a bit of shyness, stood up and walked away still completely nude.

And Jesse took time to slip in to his shorts and trousers and followed. She led him to her bedroom suite and into the bathroom. "But first we need a shower," she exclaimed and helped him out of his clothes again. Then pulled him in with her and turned on the water which had spraying heads that hit all the important parts of your body.

Elle handed him a bottle of lavender scented soap and turned her back to him saying, "First, will you wash my hair?" And he began the arduous task of washing this wonderful goddess he'd found in his travels.

-18-

As Jesse left Elle Moore's house at dawn, the first thing he did as he went out the door to his car was to quickly study the area for anyone or anything that looked suspicious. He'd left his .38 under the car seat and even though this was a gated community, he knew there were ways a devious person could get in. But all looked quiet as he drove through the still sleeping place to his hotel. The night had turned out to be a pleasant surprise to him, and now he felt good. Not only after satisfying sex but, it had felt good to share these intimate feelings with a caring woman again. It had been years since he'd felt this with his wife. Sad but true. Just as he was leaving Elle's home, as they were standing at the door saying goodnight or in this case good morning, he'd asked if he could see her again. If she would like to go out to dinner soon, and when she'd replied yes, he said he would call her later in the day and they could decide where and when to go.

Damn, he said to empty car as he drove, he wondered how Elle felt. He also wondered how someone so good looking and seemingly so normal was not attached. He'd taken a quick glance around her beautiful home and area by the ocean and knew it must have cost big bucks. When he'd exclaimed how lovely it was, she'd smiled and graciously said "thank you". But having an inquiring curiosity about peoples' portfolio's, derived from his old profession, he wondered if she'd married well and divorced smarter, or, if she'd worked hard on her own and invested wisely, or been lucky and inherited it.

Well whatever, it didn't matter to him, as he still had his own "portfolio". At the hotel, he dropped his clothes on the floor and inside of five minutes he was sound asleep between the 1000 count sleek cotton sheets, with Elle's perfume and soaps still a wonderful clinging memory. He slept soundly until almost noon then awoke to his cell phone chirping on the nearby end table. Reaching out a hand for it, he mumbled, "Hello".

"Goddam Jesse, I've been calling you for hours, where the hell have you been?" Reed, his buddy from Birch was on the line.

Jesse cleared his throat. "Hey man, sorry. I left my phone in my car. What's up?"

"Christ, you haven't called for a few days, and I was getting worried!"

"Reed, I'm still trying to figure out what's happening. Listen, did I tell you that there was a murder on that same beach, where I was when I first got fired at?" As Jesse talked, he got a water out of the small frig and downed it in almost one big swallow.

"No you didn't, who was killed?" Reed asked.

"A little seventeen year old girl training for the Olympics. And she'd been sexually assaulted and then strangled."

"Goddamn, it makes me sick, anybody in custody yet?" Reed asked.

"No, not that they're telling anyone. I had breakfast with the Chief and she's still not talking, at least not to me about it."

"I thought you were getting close to her?" Reed laughed.

"I thought so too, but then suddenly she's been pretty tight assed about it! I get she doesn't want any outside help, so I'm just doing some of my own looking around." Jesse reached for another bottle of water and opened the door to the balcony to the fresh cool ocean breeze.

"Have you found anything?" Reed wanted to know.

"Nothing new as of yet." Jesse made a stop in the bathroom as he talked. "Hey buddy, what's going on up there? And how's Ed?"

Reed laughed. "I guess you don't know, but get this. He put his car business in the hands of his manager and took off for a trip around the world. He told me he was taking Daisy O'Dell away from all the stress that killer for hire had created for her."

"You're kidding. I didn't know they had hooked up." Jesse commented.

"I guess after all the crap they had both been through, they did. He is walking on his own now."

"Well I'll be damned. Good for them. Good people." Jesse sat down in the one soft chair and put his bare feet up on an ottoman, then went on, "I guess when we had that bonfire, it satisfied those assholes across the pond?"

Reed laughed into the cell. "Yup, it's been a few years now and all is still quiet. Since there were no more sightings of Daisy, they must have figured that they got her when they blew up her car."

"It was a good ploy," Jesse remembered the worry and then the grateful lessening of it as time went by. "It's pretty quiet up there?" he asked.

"It is. We're into fall now, so the colors in the landscape are drawing car loads of sightseers through. The Woodsmen Café is swamped from morning till night and the Legion bar is stacking up their money in the back room."

Jesse had to laugh. At times he missed the town. "Buddy, have you had your boat out lately," he asked.

"I did this morning with some of the guys, we had some beers and threw some lines in the water, but we all came up empty. So really, what are you doing with your time?" Reed asked curiously.

Jesse laughed again. "Get this, I've been playing golf."

"That sounds interesting. But have you met any women?"

"Quite a few. But you know me, I play it safe." Jesse wasn't ready yet to even tell his best friend that he'd spent the last night with a woman.

"Well, be careful and watch your back." Reed added and they said goodbye.

Jesse took another shower and left his room in search of food. He hadn't eaten since the day before when he met Chief Juel for breakfast, and was starved. Since he'd gotten this new body, he didn't eat at all like he used to. Back in Birch, it was meat, potatoes and gravy too often, and over time, it had gone right to his waist. He went into the dining room at the hotel and was seated at a table for two off in the corner. Looking over the crowd there wasn't a soul he knew accept the waitress. When she saw him in her section, she smiled and hurried over.

"Good evening Mr. Ortega," she said, "What can I bring you to drink?"

Jesse didn't have to think too long and replied, "bourbon over ice, please!"

He watched her walk away and thought, "Damn, what a looker." Something strangely different had been happening to him lately and he thought about that as he waited for his drink. Damn, all of a sudden his sex drive had come to life, and all of a sudden there seemed that more than one woman stirred up his mojo.

He had a ready grin for her as she set his bourbon down on his table. "Thanks," he said.

"Name's Jesse." And after seeing her name tag on her white shirt, asked, "Okay if I call you Lola?"

"Of course, Jesse," and she stood back. "Are you staying long in town?" She asked him.

"I'm thinking of making Hilton Head my home soon."

"Well, you like it then?" She wanted to know.

"It's a beautiful place." As they made small talk, he glanced over her quickly. Damn, she was another looker. Maybe five four, a hundred and fifteen pounds. Gorgeous black hair piled high on her head and sparkling blue eyes, and also noticed she filled out her shirt quite well.

"Are you a golfer?" She asked then.

"Sometimes." He took a drink of his bourbon. "Are you a native of Hilton Head, Lola?"

She laughed. "No, I'm really from Minneapolis, Minnesota."

"Well small world, I'm from northern Minnesota!" Now, this really peaked his interest. And, he grinned again at her. "How long have you been here?"

"Well by now, I guess I am a permanent resident as I've lived here for over ten years."

"Where are you located at?" Being a retired sheriff, he still found this was important, as it told a lot about a person. All though as yet, he was still learning the different areas. When she told him where she lived, he knew right off it was considered quite a ritzy gated plantation.

"I know pretty well where you are Lola. You're right by the water too aren't you?"

"I am, sometime I'll have you over for a cocktail?" She said smiling at him.

And Jesse accepted her invitation with a grin.

-19-

"Hello, who is this?" Elle Moore asked again, annoyed. She heard a click as the line went dead, and she glared at her cell phone. As she lay in her bed this morning an uneasy feeling was edging its way into the pit of her stomach. She remembered the incident a few weeks ago when the lights had gone out while she had been taking a bath. She never did find anything wrong with her electricity to have caused that sudden outage.

Now this is silly, it was just a wrong number. If the call is for me, they'll call back in a few moments, but the cell did not ring again. It was still too early to get up on this Sunday morning, so she lay buried in the silky warmth of her flowered sheets and thought again of the evening with Jesse. She sighed with contentment as she remembered.

The summer season had flown by and the lovely colors of autumn exploded all over the Hilton Head area. Primroses, verbena, black-eyed Susan's and swamp sunflowers stood proud and tall. Flowering kale flowed over the edges of the beds with its colorful green, pink and white ruffles.

It's been over six months since I moved in here, Elle thought as she watched the waves on the rolling ocean. She had finally gotten out of bed and was sitting out on her lanai having coffee. I should be so happy now, and I would be, if it wasn't for those darn strange things that happen from time to time. Things that should normally be chalked up as circumstantial. But she would feel that same chilling question. Why and who? It would haunt her for a while and then she would push it out of her mind as nonsense, but, yet again, a niggling air of uneasiness would surface from time to time. And now, her car had broken down twice, leaving her stranded for hours waiting for help. When the tow truck driver checked her vehicle the first time, it started right off for him, but the second time now it had to be towed into a shop because one front tire had suddenly gone flat, then the second one in back followed.

"Both tires have been punctured," a mechanic told her when he called her about the problem. "Is someone trying to get even with you?"

Puzzled, Elle answered, "not that I know of."

The garage man replied, "I could see one getting cut on something sharp, but two? Nah, they've been cut on purpose!"

"Are you kidding me? As far as I know, I don't have any enemies here in town."

"At any rate, I'll need to get you all new ones, four that is." He informed her.

"Thank you, and please give me a call when you have it ready." Elle clicked off her cell. She sat for many minutes as her thoughts were in a whirl. The few months she had lived in Hilton Head, she had met several people whom she met for lunch or dinner, and had a few dates but that was all. And nobody stuck out as having a sinister air about them. But how the hell would she know anyway? She picked up her cell and dialed the police department and when a receptionist answered, she asked to be connected with Police Chief Juel Anderson, having heard there was a woman in charge.

"When did this occur," the chief asked.

"Just this afternoon. I went out to go shopping and the tires went flat, one after the other when I got out on the highway," Elle exclaimed. "The garage man says they have been punctured. I drove it last night and since then it has been parked on the side of the street where I live."

"What kind of car do you drive?"

"It's a 2014 white Mercedes."

"Okay, I'll send a detective around to see if anyone else has been targeted. And please feel free to let me know if anything else happens!"

"Thank you," Elle said and clicked off her cell. Then a thought occurred to her. She had informed Hamp that she needed to take a break from seeing him a few days earlier. Could he be behind these frightening happenings?

Maybe the police would find other neighbors had, had the same thing happen to their cars, she thought anxiously. At least then she wouldn't feel like it was totally directed at her.

Later that day, Elle stopped into Shirlee's Café. She wanted to ask Shirlee about Jesse, this great man she had met and spent the night with. She hated to think he might have done this to her car, but she needed to be practical.

Shirlee, her new friend was behind the bar busy with what looked to be a bus load of visiting senior citizens, and all seemingly wanting some brandy to warm their throat. The place hummed with conversations with background music from the sound system. Today it was pouring out Mickey Gilley's songs from his "Why Me Lord," album. Toes were tapping and a general feeling of loving everyone flowed over the place. Elle perched on a stool off to the side and soon she found herself smiling and singing along with the crowd to some good old fashioned gospel. Here in the south, the citizens loved their "church songs".

Shirlee brought over a glass of champagne and sat it down on a napkin. "Join us we're having a birthday celebration today."

"Thanks," Elle said and then asked, "Where did all these people come from?"

Shirlee laughed, "They are from my church here in Hilton Head. I invite them over for a free cocktail once a month to celebrate whoever is having a birthday, then to play bingo for several hours."

"That sounds like good advertising to me." Elle smiled.

"Believe me, it is," Shirlee nodded and hurried back over to her customers who were clamoring for refills before hurrying to tables in the overflow room for a rollicking afternoon of bingo.

After the bar quieted Shirlee came over carrying the bottle of champagne and sat down with Elle. "How are you, my friend?" She asked.

"I'm fine, Shirlee, but I need to ask you about this man I met here last week and then again last night."

"Who? Do you mean Jesse?" Shirlee smiled.

"Yes, I do. What do you know about him?"

"Actually not much. If I remember right, he's new here and from Minnesota."

"How long have you known him?" Elle persisted.

"Why?" Shirlee raised an eyebrow in question, "Elle, I don't like to talk about my customers. Is this something serious?"

"I'm not sure, but I got a little carried away last night and invited him to see my house."

"Well, I wondered why you both disappeared at about the same time. I was busy winding up my last set of the evening and didn't see you around here later. How did that go?"

"Hmm--, I'm not sure." Elle murmured.

-20-

The hotel dining room was busy this Friday morning and Jesse ordered a veggie omelet and a glass of orange juice to go with his coffee. Damn, he felt good and energized especially after the night before. Meeting Elle Moore had been his lucky day. Not only for the intimacy they'd shared, but for the feelings he had become aware of lately. Now after this wholesome breakfast he was going to go out to the beach again and see if anybody looked suspicious.

"Thank you Lola for the delicious breakfast, I hope your day goes well for you," he said to her when he paid his check.'

"And, your day as well." Lola smiled at him and winked as he went out the door.

Well, that sure made him feel special. As he was walking back to his room, it finally dawned on him that aside for his new golfing buddies his acquaintances were all women so far.

That of course made him smile, as previously this hadn't been happening for decades now, as he was accustomed to only being greeted as Sheriff Ortega, or as his wife's husband. He grinned at no one in particular as he got in the elevator as it felt pretty damn good!

Back in his room, he donned a t-shirt, shorts, cap, and sun glasses. Then shoved books and bottles of water in a bag and took off. Today he was going back to the first complex he'd stayed at and the place where those first shots had just missed his head while he was walking along the water's edge. This was also where that young Olympic hopeful had been assaulted and killed. Now, several weeks had gone by and he wanted to take a look around.

He hid his car in another close by lot and walked over carrying a sand chair and his bag. As he came over the dunes covered with the tall sea oats, the sun blazing over the ocean waves caught his breath. It never ceased to amaze him in all its glory even after seeing it so many times already. He quickly scanned the area and found a space where he had a good view of the people coming to the beach to walk or to suntan. Today he wore a straw hat with curled up sides and with his dark glasses he had a rakish look, changing his look again, as he settled in.

The beach was crowded and Jesse took careful notice of each and every single person, and carefully scanned the groups. To the casual observer, he portrayed the look of a relaxed sunbather intent on a good book, but here again behind his dark glasses, his searching observance kept the whole area under scrutiny. Time slowed down and the oceans hum totally hushed conversations as he stretched out in the chair. Several hours passed and he felt a nap coming on.

Then suddenly a lone individual walked into his line of vision and caught his eye. Jesse studied this man's gait. The thing that alarmed him was he was striding along trying to look casual, but Jesse could see by the angle of his head he was scanning the beach scene ahead of him through his dark glasses. The same way Jesse did. He was wearing white shorts and was bare and tanned on top. He seemed to be six feet tall and weigh around two hundred and looked to have dirty blond colored hair.

God almighty, Jesse thought, as the individual came closer. He leaned further back in his chair and his heart pumped hard in his chest as the man came within twenty yards from him and then passed.

Jesse turned to casually watch, and then he quickly tossed his things in his bag, leaving his sand chair in the dunes, and began to follow at a safe distance. The man did not look back and Jesse lost himself in the pack of walkers. And just to make sure the man wouldn't recognize him, Jesse quickly replaced his straw hat with a baseball cap and this time put on mirrored dark glasses.

A good thirty minutes passed as the two men walked along, the stranger ahead of Jesse by thirty or forty yards. Then the man came to a sudden stop and dropped down on a blanket where a woman lay sunning, wearing the barest of bikinis.

As Jesse got closer, he turned to watch the water but could see in his peripheral vision, as he passed by the man was kissing the red haired woman as they lay close together. Then he heard the woman's laugh which sounded more like a girls giggle.

There was just something about this man! God almighty, Jesse felt it in his gut the minute he'd seen him covertly scanning the beaches. Was he just wistfully lusting over the scene, or was the bastard searching?

Jesse walked on then and found a large washed up tree limb and sat down. After another twenty minutes or so, he saw the couple get up and walk with arms around each other to the parking lot where they got into a white jeep which she drove. Too late to follow, as Jesse's car was over in another lot, all he could do was memorize the license number. He hurried over to his car and got out his cell. But who the hell could he call? He didn't have the outlets available here since he had retired, but he got his buddy Reed on his cell.

"Hey Reed," he said, "Could you run this plate for me?"

"Sure, what's the number?" And it took several minutes for the exchange and for Reed to make the call. "While we wait, tell me what you've got?" Reed exclaimed.

"I just ran across someone who looks suspicious and I could be wrong. There's just something about the guy!"

"Yeah? Where did you find him?" Reed wanted to know.

"On the beach. I've been watching and following him. Then he rode off with a redhead in a white Jeep."

"Her wheels?" Reed asked.

"Don't know. We'll soon see who owns it." Jesse started his Buick and drove out of the parking lot which belonged to the large Regency Hotel. He was on his way back to his own hotel for a shower.

Jesse and Reed exchanged the latest news and compared weather as they waited for a return call from Reed's "go to" person. Then Reed got the news and clicked Jesse back on.

"Here it is, the Jeep is a 2014 model registered to an Amy Paulson. Address is listed at 6281 Florida St. NW, Hilton Head, South Carolina."

"Okay thanks Reed, I'll get back to you," Jesse assured his friend and clicked off his cell. He turned on his GPS for the address and within ten minutes he drove up to a gated complex of town houses and single residents, where a person sat in a small enclosure checking residents in.

Well hell, the place didn't look that rich, Jesse grumbled. What now? If he hadn't had to run to get his Buick he could have followed the Jeep. Now he didn't know if it had come back here, or even if the Amy Paulson listed as the driver of the Jeep was really the redhead seen on the beach with this man.

-21-

Jesse grumbled as he sat in his Buick after coming to another locked and gated community. Did everybody live behind inaccessible fences? He'd just spent hours sweating on the beach hoping to catch this guy that might be his stalker/shooter but now had lost him completely. If he hadn't had to get his Buick parked a block away, he wouldn't have lost the one and only clue he'd found so far to this damnable mystery as to who the hell was playing with his life. He could have followed that damn white Jeep. Now he didn't know if the couple in it had come back here to this address or even if the Amy Paulson listed as the driver of the Jeep was really the woman he'd seen on the beach.

The complex was called the Southern Belle and did appear to have all the bells and whistles from what he could see from outside the gate. Palms, bushes and succulents had looked well cared for, but of course, here in the south everything grew in wild blazing abandonment and had to be pruned back constantly or else the foliage would get out of control fast.

He parked across from the gate, next to a Dairy Queen and a stand of palm trees and shrubbery for cover. It was a busy place with couples, kids and teenagers.

As Jesse sat outside the gate waiting for the white Jeep to come out, he thought again of the night he'd spent with Elle Moore. He wondered if she had felt anything special about their love-making. Now to him, it had been really earth shaking, but then he hadn't experienced that for years. But of course she was a beautiful woman and no doubt had quite a few suitors after her. Well hell, now he was depressed.

Jesse sat listening to the radio and the announcer's spiel about the weather, competitions coming up on the many golf courses, car sales and restaurant specials. At the mention of food he suddenly felt his stomach growl and remembered he hadn't eaten much so far today. Now he was depressed and hungry. But he'd just have to suck it up and wait and not leave since he had gotten so far already, but he remembered he did have another bottle of water left in his beach bag. And, finding it he guzzled it down and felt better.

Time went by as he sat in his car. Thankfully, he sat under the trees in the shade as the southern sun was hot, but he had the windows down and the usual trade winds off the ocean cooled the island even from a few blocks over. Suddenly, his cell vibrated in his shirt pocket and he hurriedly clicked in. Reed was calling him back.

"Hey Jesse," he said and asked, "Did you find anything?"

Jesse was glad of the interruption but kept his voice down. "I found her place and am sitting here waiting to see if the Jeep is here. It's a gated complex so I don't even know if the guy came here or not."

"Oh yeah, I remember. I was there a few times years ago when Lindy lived there. But if someone really wants to get into most of those locked communities, you know all you have to do is go in through the nearest beach. But of course it's not something most would think off." Reed offered.

"Well hell, I'm not going to do that. There are alligators all over the place here. Ugly looking creatures and they scare the shit out of me."

"That too," Reed said. "But listen, if and when you see this character again snap a picture of him on your cell. I got to thinking we could do some checking with it through the state and nation wide catalog of known offenders."

Jesse's stomach tightened over remembering that. God, he should have thought of that earlier and had his cell ready, but he'd turned it to vibrate and stuffed it in his beach bag.

"I forgot about that."   Jesse mumbled. "But thanks for the reminder.

"How long have you been sitting there." Reed asked.

Jesse glanced at his watch and saw several hours had gone by and he was getting restless. What the hell was this turkey doing, it didn't take this long for sex. Then he had a thought, maybe the guy lived there too!

"God almighty, Reed," he said then, "I was thinking that he would be there only for a short time, but now, I realize he could live there too. He probably won't come out until tomorrow."

"Yup, that's true. Listen buddy, I've got to take off now, but give me a call later." And Reed clicked off.

Jess sat for a while longer but now he tapped a finger on the steering wheel of his car as he waited for something to happen. And he had his cell ready.

It was nearing late afternoon and the sun was still beating out a temp of 98 degrees, but, now it had moved and was shining directly on the car as well.

Well hell, he grumbled and started the car and turned on the A/C full blast. Should he give it up? Well, maybe he could get cooled off and wait some more. After all, where was he going anyway?

Something prompted him to stay out a little longer, and after getting cooled off, he moved the car over slightly under another copse of palms. Now he had an even better view of the gate so he'd give it another hour. Then for sure he had to get some food.

The time dragged and he even thought he might put his head back on the top of the car seat and rest his eyes for just a minute, when the white Jeep came flying out the gate. He sat up, started the car and slowly turned onto the street several cars behind it. By now the sun had gone down and everyone had put their lights on. And the Jeep had gone by so fast, Jesse couldn't be sure if there was more than the driver in the vehicle.

Well, now something was finally happening and Jesse's actions were measured. He needed to be careful and not let his Buick be seen, just in case, he'd been made previously, but he didn't think he had been so far.

Jesse kept well back from the Jeep as now they were on the main street of Hilton Head which was the highway that also led from one end of the island, which, incidentally was twelve miles long, eventually to a long bridge and over the International Waterway and on to Savannah Georgia. This was downtown Hilton Head and extended for miles with restaurants, hotels and shops, and who shared the area with gated arches into plantations of condos, apartments and single family homes.

Jesse had gotten familiar with the landmarks around the town earlier and now saw the Jeep was heading for the side of the island where the elite lived in huge mansions. Here again, he knew he couldn't drive in, but he had gone on an excursion one day when he'd first gotten to the island and gotten a brief look in to the place and saw the awesome homes. Now ahead, he saw the Jeep cruise through the gate and after a brief stop saw it disappear inside and out of sight.

Damn, he drove by feeling pissed and frustrated. But at least now he had two places to watch, he grudgingly thought to himself. And there didn't seem to make sense to watch and wait any longer tonight as the guy must live there, and he needed a shower and food.

Back at his hotel, Jesse stood under the hot and then cooler water and let it wash over his stiff and tired body. He wasn't used to sitting in one spot anymore and had missed his daily walk that morning. Tomorrow he needed to get out early for his usual three mile hike. Tonight however, he wanted a nice big steak and a baked potato, but maybe not the sour cream and cheese like he used to enjoy up in Birch. Soon he was ready wearing a long sleeve white shirt, open at the collar and rolled at the cuffs. He slipped on a pair of black linen slacks and of course went sockless in his black tasseled loafers and finally with a spritz of Armani, he was ready. As he checked his appearance in a mirror even he had to admit he looked hot. He laughed on the way out.

-22-

Elle Moore liked her new home and the town of Hilton Head even though these bizarre things happening to her lately gave her the "heebie-jeebies", as her mother would have exclaimed. As she walked through the house, she studied the paintings on the living room wall.

Jesus, it gave her goose-bumps, where had those two new ones come from? There had been fourteen contemporary oil paintings left unclaimed on the walls when Elle had bought the house, and then suddenly two more had been added. Had someone come in when she was sleeping? Damn she forgot, she should have mentioned this to the Police Chief when she had reported the situations concerning her car. She'd call back today as they could be connected! But she'd get the locks changed again and then see what happened. And having that accomplished by evening she showered, dried and curled her hair, dressed in a white jumpsuit and high heeled sandals, then got in her car and drove downtown.

One thing she loved about the town was the outdoor lighting at night which gave it an exciting carnival appearance after dusk. She drove down to Harbor Town where an original light house still stood. But of course, now it housed a bustling cafe with a souvenir shop hugging the water's edge. She saw the area also offered permanent metal benches for the weary shopper to sit and relax and gaze at the sights. She parked and went to the café called Harbor Place, which was an outdoor café that extended out over the water. Tonight a group of musicians featuring guitarist, Dan T sat off to a side and played soft and sexy jazz. A tuxedo clad maître'd greeted her and led her out on the deck, to a candle lit table for two. Glass walls; four feet high housed the room and had seating for approximately fifty people under the stars, with another large room just inside.

Elle loved this place. She had come several times before and had a light lunch of a salad and fresh caught seafood. Tonight however, she had decided to just have a cocktail or two and relax and enjoy the mystery of the ocean. She could do this also at home because her house faced the dunes and the ocean, but here on the deck it was the next best thing to being out on it. She asked for a champagne cocktail and relaxed, and ordered her thoughts to be gentle and positive.

Lights from passing yachts of varying sizes lit up the view out on the water, and the huge ships held her attention as to what they carried in their cavernous bellies. After her second cocktail, Elle was in a mellow mood and for a minute, gazed around the many tables. There was a small area for dancing and some people were gyrating to the tunes. She eyed them. Tonight she felt like dancing and almost got up by herself to bop to the many moves when to her delight a man came over and extended his hand.

"May I?" He asked and smiled.

"I'd love to." She replied and stood. He took her in his arms and they danced body to body, not saying a word to break the magic they were feeling until the music stopped.

As he led her back to her table, he asked, "Are you alone?"

When Elle answered she was he asked if she would like another drink?

"Thanks but no. I've just enjoyed my limit. But I could go for an iced tea?"

"Well, then I'll send one over." He kissed her hand and walked away in to the maze of tables on the deck. And Elle sat down at hers.

Well, that was strange, I just expected him to want to join me here, she thought to herself. And within minutes a waiter brought her a lovely tall glass of iced tea. She tasted it, and then set it down. And feeling rejected, after several more minutes she stood up. Damn, now she was pissed. And not even looking around to see where the stranger might be seated, she walked out. Well, too bad for you she consoled herself, you just missed out on a good evening of dancing and good company.

It was getting onto eleven and not one to bar hop by herself she decided to go home and make a sandwich and watch some television. But as she walked out to her car, some movement caught the corner of her eye. In a quick glance, she was sure she saw her dance partner, that same man sitting in a nearby vehicle, quickly slide down in the seat and disappear from sight. She hurried to hers, got in and took off. Spooked and speeding out of the area she breathed relief when her home came in to view. She parked quickly and ran inside and not turning on any lights, she stood by a window and watched to see if anyone had followed her. She thought the vehicle had been small and in a light color. Nothing like that appeared on her street, so after several more minutes Elle gave it up. But not before she double checked the new locks on her doors and windows, and then finally got in to bed.

The ringing of her cell awoke her the next morning.

"Elle, good morning," She heard. "This is Jesse, but am I calling too early?"

"Well, yes and no," she murmured seeing the time on the bedside table said eight a.m.

"Sorry, should I call back later?" He asked.

"Give me thirty minutes and I'll have my coffee ready!" And she threw back the covers on her bed and stood up, then went out to the kitchen and got the coffee pot going. She turned on the remote that slid back the wall of glassed doors that opened out to the lanai. It was another perfect day and the breeze off the ocean aired the house. When the coffee was ready Elle poured a giant sized cup and took up her cell and went out to enjoy the morning sun. She had slipped on a short pink sundress and ran a brush through her red hair on her way to the kitchen, so she relaxed now and exactly thirty minutes later, Jesse's phone call woke up the morning.

"Got your coffee?" He asked.

"I have. I'm outside on my lanai right now. God, it's another beautiful day!" Elle remarked. "I see you're an early bird." She said to him.

"In my former life I was, and still am I guess. It's hard to break old habits."

"I've found that out too. However, mine was just the opposite. I like to work late into the night so I usually sleep later."

"Sorry," he seemed to hesitate then.

"What's up, Jesse?" Elle asked.

"I'm wondering if you would like to go out to dinner Saturday night?" He asked.

Well, she sure would. After their time in bed together, she hoped she hadn't been just a one night stand, and would have certainly regretted it if he never called her.

"I'd love to. What time?" She asked and they agreed seven o'clock would be great.

"I'm wondering if you're familiar with Shelter Cove. There's a great restaurant on the wharf there that has wonderful food I've heard."

"I've been there for shopping and lunch, but never for dinner. I'd love it Jesse!"

- 23-

Jesse stood at the bar in Shirlee's Café and savored his Kentucky blend bourbon. The evening was in full swing with Shirlee at the baby grand belting out an Aretha Franklin love song. It was Friday night and Hilton Head Island was vibrating with tourists and residents alike all out enjoying a warm autumn evening. This time back in Birch Lake, Jesse remembered the town would be busy with high school homecoming football games and teen dances. In the years his son, Jesse Junior, was a hormone restless teenager that time had flown by, busy with cars and girls. Then suddenly it seemed the kid had grown up and graduated from college, and then only called home every week or so. But it was gratifying to know that he had a good job as an engineer with a huge company in Minneapolis, and that he seemed to be getting along just fine, even without his old man at his side to help make his decisions.

Damn, he was getting maudlin in his thoughts. But God almighty, Jesse brushed a hand over his face, he did miss the old times back there from time to time. Then feeling a brush at his elbow, he turned to see Chief Juel Anderson smiling at him.

"Well hello Mr. Ortega. Nice seeing you here tonight." She said and raised a hand for his.

"Chief," Jesse managed over his surprise. First at seeing her here out on the night, and then, that she seemed pleased to see him. "How are you?" He asked.

"I'm fine and enjoying the evening." Then turning to a man standing beside her, she said, "Scot, I'd like you to meet a new tourist to our fair city, this is Jesse Ortega. Jesse this is Scot Fairbanks, our mayor." And the two men shook hands as each took each other's measure.

"Would you like to join us at our table Jesse," the chief asked politely while Scot looked on with a stiff smile.

Jesse declined just as politely. "But thanks," he added, "Maybe another time." And he watched them tread their way back to a table, the guys arm possessively around her waist. What a phony, Jesse mumbled under his breath at the guy's apparent distain at the thought of sharing time with a tourist. He had to admit though the chief looked pretty damn good in her dress up clothes.

He took another swallow of his bourbon and out of habit scanned the faces of the party imbibing crowd. Most of them were couples, groups of women, and some single individuals at the bar. He looked them over, and didn't let his eyes linger on any one person. But trained to quickly memorize a face, he did just that. There was one guy, sitting alone drinking something that looked like a coke, who triggered his radar. So as not to seem interested, Jesse turned his back for a moment and made a casual comment about the weather to the group of women who sat next to him as he stood at the bar. After a moment he turned sideways to check out of his peripheral vision and saw the man still sat seemingly engrossed in the entertainment. And in that glance Jesse took him to be in his late thirties, of Latin descent, with muscled shoulders and a thick neck.

Shirlee had just finished her set amid applause and made her way through the crowd to his side. He watched her greet friends along the way.

"Thank you for coming, Jesse," she said smiling at him and touched his sleeve.

"My pleasure, you've got a packed house, I see."

"And I thank God, people want to come." She looked around and grinned at acquaintances.

Tonight she was wearing a black jumpsuit with sparkling jewels in her ears and at her neck. Her hair was pulled back in a sleek pony tail.

"Can I get you a refill?" Shirlee asked.

"Thanks, I'm fine. But you can sing one of my favorite songs though, if you have time." Jesse offered.

"Okay, name it."

"It's called 'The Tennessee Waltz'. An oldie that brings me back to simpler times."

Shirlee smiled at him. "Oh, I can tell you're just a softy at heart. That's one of the most frequently requested songs I get asked to do."

"Really!" Jesse commented. "Then I'm not too old fashioned? But actually I like all styles of music. Rock and roll tops the list however."

"You sound like a well-rounded connoisseur of music." Shirlee said.

"I guess so." As Jesse talked, he turned and quickly checked out the suspicious looking guy. But he seemed to be in a conversation with the man on the bar stool next to him. Well hell, he could be wrong.

"Do you live here on the island?" Turning back, he asked Shirlee.

"I do. I live over on the Hilton Head Plantation. It's one of the oldest areas here." Shirlee smiled and murmured thanks to the bartender as she placed a large glass of water on the bar for her. After drinking some, she asked, "Jesse, are you planning on staying here?"

"I might." Of course, he had not told her about someone taking those shots at him. But he was not going to be run out of town by this asshole!

"Have you been out on the water yet?" She wondered.

"No, but I'm thinking of looking into one of the day charters I've seen advertised."

"You should. There's good deep sea fishing. Also, if you just like to canoe there's inlets nearby that are safe."

Jesse took another quick look at the guy at the bar across from him. And this time, Jesse caught him just turning away after looking his way.

But he kept their conversation going and asked, "Do you have any recommendations as to where I might find some property to buy if I decide to stay?" Jesse asked.

"You know, it's a buyer's market out here now Jesse. I haven't kept up but I have a friend who is a broker. If you want I can give you his name."

"Okay, thanks." Jesse nodded.

Shirlee checked the time. "Sorry Jesse, I have to get back. But please stay." And with a smile went back to her baby grand where she ran her fingers over the keys and the hum of conversations stopped as she went into the song he had requested.

Jesse smiled, then finished his drink and decided to leave. Now he'd see if the asshole at the bar came out to follow him. He got in his car and watched, but when the guy he thought looked suspicious didn't rush out, Jesse knew he had been wrong. Damn, he'd been ready to give him a ride of his life!

Back at his hotel, he turned on the television to watch Jimmy Kimmel.

-24-

One thing he couldn't stand was people trying to run away from their actions and hide far away in a new metropolis. The way he saw it was if you took a life you better be ready to pay up with your own.

Carlo Prada was considered a multi-millionaire player in his country. He was used to riches, guns and women. After his junior and high school days he had gone to college and had been in the top five percentile of his class. He was handsome in a rugged way that fit his swagger. Black hair, brown eyes and flashing white teeth got your attention when he came in to a room. He could turn on all his charm when he wanted to, and then turn it off when he wanted to keep a low profile.

Real-estate, restaurants, pornography, banks, guns and drugs were just a few of his family's holdings to name. He came from a generation's old, family of ten children and everyone was involved in one of their businesses. And every one lived in beautiful houses. Five boys and five girls, all married with families, except Carlo. He had a beautiful home as well, but his was a bachelor pad with leather furniture, thick carpets and a swimming pool. He had a chef on call and a thick little black book of the telephone numbers of his many women. Most of whom, were anxious to please a rich single man.

In those early teenage days, however, Carlo was forced to work in one of their restaurants, first as a dishwasher, a bus boy and then finally as a waiter. He was too young by law to serve liquor but he managed that by having one of his older brothers carry the tray of cocktails to his tables. He learned at a very young age how to use his good looks to his advantage and crammed his pockets with cash after his shifts.

Carlo had a younger brother who had gotten most of their mother's love. A scholar with his nose always in a book, now CEO of their banks in their fair city. Carlo had been born first and always considered himself to be the older brother and therefore boss. So he took credit for his little brother's jobs around home and took pleasure in scaring him into silence. When he became twenty-one he came of age to share in the families vast riches and he promptly set himself up in style. From then on, Carlo did only what he wanted. However, there was one thing that he had promised his aged grandmother he would do and that was to bring one man to his knees. One man, who had been responsible for killing two of her beloved sons, and then was somehow behind the loss of her two grandsons who had drowned in his lake! A devil's handiwork!

And, now, she had threatened to take away his riches if he didn't show her his love by finally fulfilling his promise. And Carlo Prada had put his plan into action!

-25-

Elle stepped into a warm bath. Tonight was going to be a special time, Jesse had said and she was looking forward to seeing him again. Her cell phone rang then as she hung up her robe and leaning over to check the caller saw a new and strange number. Someone from Savannah, she saw. Well hell, she didn't have time to find out right now who it was either.

She stepped in to the perfumed warm bubbles and slid down in the water up to her chin. She turned the Jacuzzi on and lay back and relaxed. Mozart played on her sound system and she closed her eyes.

Lord, this was close to heaven, she thought. Then suddenly the lights went off and the music stopped.

Again, just like before! Only now whenever she took a bath or shower she would light some candles just in case this same incident wouldn't catch her unawares as before. But it still scared the heck out of her and she immediately got out and grabbed a big towel. She ran over and locked the bathroom door, then grabbed up her cell and called 911.

"I think there's someone in my house," she whispered again to a dispatcher. "Can you send someone over right away?   I'm locked in my bathroom!"

"Okay, give me your address. But how will the officers get in to check?"

Elle sucked in her breath, but then right away said, "On the patio, tell them to look under the pot of red flowers on the table for the key. I'll wait in here until they knock on this door. Oh hurry please!"

She dropped the bath towel on the floor and tied a robe around herself and sat down on the dressing table stool to wait. She thought she heard footsteps on the wooden floors in the living room, or maybe it was the dining room. She couldn't be sure. Maybe it was her imagination! Oh God, what was taking the police so long? She stood impatiently and then paced, but she couldn't go very far in the small room. What the hell could she do if someone tried to open the door right now, she thought wildly. She had nothing in there that she could use for protection if someone broke it down. And then suddenly, as she sat in the bathroom, something edged itself into her thoughts again.

Several weeks ago, she had broken the relationship off with Hamp after that last date she'd had with him. He had seemed overly interested in her financial investments, and only seemed to irritate her lately so she had told him she didn't want to see him again. He'd gotten pissed, and now she wondered if he was responsible for this episode and also for the time before when the lights went off. It took the police ten minutes to get there and by the time one knocked on the bathroom door Elle was a wreck.

"Miss Moore, it's Deputy Jordan. We checked your house and around the outside and it doesn't appear that anything has been disturbed. You can unlock the door now."

She unlocked the door as he continued, "I was here the last time, and I would suggest you have the wiring checked. There might be something there causing your electricity to go off." And the police left.

Hell, she just didn't know! And now she was all stressed out.

Five minutes after they left, Jesse rang her doorbell. "Hello gorgeous," he said and stepped in to her foyer. Then he took another look at her. "Am I early?" he asked and looked at his watch.

"No, I had a situation and had to call the police." She tucked the collar in on the robe.

Jesse looked alarmed. "Why, what happened?"

"I thought someone was in the house!" Elle exclaimed, her voice still somewhat shaky.

"Someone broke in? Are you okay?" He stepped up and peered closely at her.

"Yes, I'm okay. I don't know what's going on and this is the second time this same thing has happened to me."

"Tell me about it," Jesse encouraged and led her over to a bench in the foyer.

And Elle went on to tell him about the first time this had happened and then again, this evening. "I don't know if it has something to do with this house or if this is directed at me for something." Elle said and brushed the hair away from her flushed face.

Jesse cleared his throat and out of habit went into his investigator cop mode. "Can you think of anyone purposely wanting to scare you?" He asked.

Elle blew out a breath, and then shook her head. "But there could be one. I may be way out in left field, but there is someone I could have irritated enough to where they might want to strike out at me."

"Who," Jesse asked, "a girlfriend, a neighbor?"

"No, it was a man I'd been dating. I broke it off and I know he got angry."

"Mad enough to do this sort of thing?" Jesse leaned in closer. "Is he a local, or a tourist?" He asked wanting to know.

Elle stood up. "Jesse, give me fifteen minutes to get dressed and ready, and we can leave. I can fill you in more then, over a cocktail."

He stood as well and they went into the living room. "I'll wait here, but take your time." And Elle hurried to her bedroom and closed the door. Her hands still shook as she opened drawers and closets. On second thought, maybe she should stay home, she thought nervously. But then maybe something else would happen. So she quickly did her make-up and hair, and then slipped on a white sleeveless dress and sandals. Twenty minutes later she came out of the bedroom.

"Wow," Jesse exclaimed saying again, "Now you look even more gorgeous!"

"Thank you, I'm still feeling somewhat shaky, but I'm looking forward to a nice glass of wine."

"Take a minute and a deep breath, Elle. Here sit down, we don't have to hurry."

Elle sat down on a couch and leaned her head back on the top. After a few minutes, she sat up and said, "Thanks Jesse, I'm fine now."

They left her house after deciding to go to Shirlee's Café down on the water front in Hilton Head.

Elle hadn't noticed a tan colored van with a sign on it that read "Handyman For Hire," follow them as they left her neighborhood, but Jesse had kept his eyes on it as he drove.

He exclaimed, "We've got a tail!"

"Who in the world—," and Elle started to turn around in her seat to look. But Jesse hurriedly put a hand out to stop her.

"Wait, don't turn around. I can see him." He said as they drove, "we'll just see what he does. I've got the license number."

After a few minutes, Elle, whispered, "Is he still behind us?"

"Yes, but we'll see if he follows us into Shirlee's." And when they turned into the parking lot, he sped on by. "There he's gone, but hang on." And Jesse did a quick turn-around and they were out on the street again, this time following him.

The traffic at this hour was heavy due to a candlelight parade getting ready to take place later in the downtown area. The local high school band was tuning up as they sat on the lawn of a park and floats were beginning to arrive to line up and as yet the streets weren't blocked off. Apparently the van driver wasn't aware that now he was being followed and took his time meandering through the streets. Then he slid to a stop and went in and parked in the lot at the bar called the Snake Pit. Jesse drove in right behind him. He quickly parked saying softly, "Elle, lock the doors and don't get out!"

Outside the bar, Jesse ran up quickly behind the guy and flung his arm around his neck and got the sucker in a head lock, shutting off his air. Then he kicked his feet out from under him and they both went down. Jesse landing right on top of him.

"Son of a bitch," the guy swore. "Get off me, fucker!"

"Nope, can't do it." Jesse yelled. "Who the hell are you?"

"Christ, who the hell are you?" The guy underneath swore some more.

"I'm a friend of Elle's!" Jesse said not loosening his hold on the guy.

"Well, get the hell off me or I will arrest you. I'm a cop!"

"Jesus Christ, what the hell are you doing following us?" Jesse growled and then slowly let him up.

The man stood up and brushed off his clothes. "Goddamn, I'm trying to find out why someone is stalking Miss Moore!"

"Well, it isn't me." Jesse took out his wallet and handed it to him. He still had his sheriff's shield in plain view, although the dates on it had expired. "Here's my ID, now let me see yours!"

"Yeah?" The guy looked at Jesse's ID. "Well I'll be fucked, you're the heat too?" He tossed it back to Jesse and held out his own wallet.

It didn't take Jesse long to see the guy was legit after comparing the picture next to his license. Although Jesse still didn't like him.

"Okay then," Jesse said and shook the guys hand. He reached over and brushed at a speck of dirt on the man's shirt. "Sorry buddy, keep up the good work." All this took about ten minutes and he hurried back to Elle who was sitting and waiting patiently unaware in his encounter with the driver of the van.

"Did you find him? What happened?" She asked, anxiety in her voice when he climbed in the car after knocking on the window for her to unlock the door.

"You won't believe this, but the guy is a cop and was following us." He didn't say anything to her about the scuffle.

"Us, why?" Elle asked.

Jesse laughed, "He wanted to know who I was."

"You, does he think--?" And she just stared at him.

-26-

Jesse left Elle's bed at around three a.m. after their enjoyable dinner and evening spent at Shirlee's Café. They'd come back to her house and had a liqueur out on the lanai and watched the stars. This time they had gone into her bedroom and took their time undressing, then got into bed. They'd kissed and caressed, and then Elle had reached over for her new bottle of oil.

"This is called Rose Orchids," she whispered and took off the cap and warmed some in her hands. And, after exchanging massages the next few hours were blissful, and Jesse had to really force himself to get out of her bed and go back to his hotel. But he had things to do.

First of all, as he left Elle's place he wanted to see if he had another tail. And sure enough he did! And he took whoever it was, on a merry go around until he lost it and then finally got back to his hotel.

But was it the detectives who were watching Elle's house after her calls about her home being invaded or was it someone following him?

The next morning he got another disguise together and grabbed his sand chair and his bag of books and magazines and headed out for another beach. He wanted to see if the white Jeep might be around again, that had disappeared into that locked plantation. He found a good spot to sit, where he could see the faces of the strollers and also could check over the sunbathers through his dark glasses. He had a blue baseball cap pulled down over his dark hair, and by now he was as tan as he wanted to be so he used a 40 sun block over his face and chest. After getting greased up he sat back in his chair and pulled out a magazine to supposedly read.

As he sat, his gaze hidden behind the dark glasses, he saw quite a few sexual adventures being played out. Like the couple lying side by side a short distance away, their hands hidden under towels plainly massaging each other. And another couple sitting together, her inside his legs, actually the smile on her face gave it all away. Jesse had to smile at the naiveté of the sun worshippers.

It had been a few days now since any shots had threatened his life. The thought occurred to him that maybe that's all there was to it. That whoever had been toying with him had given up and moved on. As he sat, he searched each face for some familiarity, something that would trigger his memory as to maybe this was someone he might have known or just met who was playing these games with him. But damn, nothing came to him. Turning a page from time to time he looked like he could have been an retiree or college professor taking a sabbatical, and not, a retired sheriff, looking for this asshole who had been taking shots at his head.

Jesse took a bottle of water out of his beach bag and then just as he raised his head to savor the goodness as it cooled his parched throat his glance collided with another man's stare who had just sat down on the sand. Something about him--. And to test the stranger's intentions, after a few minutes Jesse gathered his things, stood and walked away quickly, purposely through a crowd of people playing and watching a volleyball game. After a short distance he turned and looked back, and the guy had vanished. But was he behind him somewhere? As Jesse was just about to his car in the next parking lot, he felt the air shift as a silenced bullet flew past his head and heard the ping as it hit a window of a another car. He dropped to the ground.

He lay for minutes then jumped up and ran for the car, got in and sped out of there. Several miles away he stopped and took his frustration out on the steering wheel. But now at last he might have a suspect. But Jesus, what the hell was this about? Why can't I catch up with the fucker?

After he had calmed down he slipped on a shirt and stopped at a coffee shop and went in and sat down to think. He had to go back to that strange feeling he had earlier of something about the guy he had seen at the beach, that seemed familiar in some way.

But what the hell was it? He just couldn't put a finger on it. But goddamn, it felt close. Was it something about his face? His looks in general?

Jesse drained his first French roast and got a refill. At least in here he could keep an eye on who came in so he let his thoughts ramble.

In his past, as a cop on the force in one of the northern towns and then later, after moving to Birch Lake and running for county sheriff, and being elected, he had known many crooks and hoodlums, and had put dozens of them away. But mostly small stuff, however, the only noteworthy case he had ever had was the Lindy Lewis catastrophe involving the biggest drug dealers known. The time two brothers from over the Mexican border had been killed in his jurisdiction, and then also the same area where two more young gay men had been found drowned in his own Birch Lake. But that had been a few years ago. Since then he had retired from his sheriff duties and left the area. The only one who knew his actual whereabouts was his friend, Reed Conners, and he wouldn't disclose that to anybody.

Jesse finished his second cup of coffee and by now he had shifted into high gear. He stopped at a take-out and got a sandwich and drove over to the locked plantation where he had seen the guy driving the white Jeep disappear into. He parked across from the entrance by a cluster of trees and sat back to wait and watch.

-27-

Carlo Prada got in his Maserati which was a sea foam green, foreign sports model, the same color of the ocean at certain times of the day and sped out of the gated plantation. As a member of the prestigious family who owned the whole tip of the island in Hilton Head, his place was a town house among the vacation homes and condos in their gated plantation, where the security was airtight 24/7.

The main, oldest house had been the summer home there for decades and had housed the original family of three daughters, whose father had been a member of the underworld. They actually all lived across the border in Monterrey, Mexico and as the family grew, they acquired more and more real estate in Hilton Head, South Carolina. The family built the Catholic Church there in Hilton Head and the talk was they kept the church of God available for their own people to come to and be liberated of their sins.

Carlo Prada introduced himself around the town as Carl Rogers, where he spent as much time there as he did at his home across the border. He did not work at any of the family businesses, but collected a huge check every year from them. He slept late and sun-tanned, and if one of his female friends wanted to dally away the afternoon, he would book a suite at one of the five star hotels on the water. As a narcissist, he'd spend time on the beach perfecting his tan as he always wore white. He had a valet who came in every week to take care of his wardrobe, here and away.

Carlo Prada was having fun playing a cat and mouse game with a certain executioner from the north, as Jesse Ortega, had to pay for taking the lives of his two brothers and his two young nephews. But Carlo was getting tired of trying to appease his cranky old grandmother's threat of taking away his yearly millions if he didn't find the man responsible and make him pay with his life. Time was running out, she had threatened.

She had also ordered Carlo that while he was there in Hilton Head, to locate another member of the family, Mariah Mercado, his niece and a promising young artist.

And Carlo Prada was pissed about being threatened!

-28-

Jesse Ortega, retired sheriff from Birch Lake, Minnesota, liked the town of Hilton Head SC. It had the colorful vegetation that he admired in the north, naturally of a different theme here, but it was abundant around every corner. The weather was beautiful in the autumn with warm temps and cool trade winds off the ocean. For the first time in decades he was not dreading a cold and blustery winter to get through. It would get chilly here over the early new year but only for a month or two, he had been told and without snow banks to clear, he could get through those cooling trends like a breeze.

He'd met a number of people, albeit mostly all women, so he figured he'd go back to that same golf course and see if he could find those old dudes he'd played golf with. He wanted to get away from the tag game he seemed to have wandered in to. And too, maybe if he stepped away from it all, he could see things from another angle and figure out how to untangle himself from the interest of the cops in Elle's trouble and the nut job trying to shoot his brains out. How he ever got himself into this debauchery of his good name was beyond him.

The minute he stepped into the pro shop on the golf course, he saw his same three buddies standing off to the side looking hopefully for a fourth to join their group. When they recognized their old pal Jesse step in, they immediately brightened their smiles and almost tripped over each other getting to his side.

"Our friend is here!" The one in the same orange pants exclaimed. "We need you for a foursome, Jesse!"

"Will you join us?" Another old guy asked. Another pushed his way over, "We've gotten real good now cuz we play every day!" And they circled around Jesse expectantly.

And he was glad to see all these guys again. "Thanks for waiting for me. Let's go," he said while picking up his bag of clubs and leading the way out the pro shop while his buddies clattered after him dragging theirs.

Now as he watched their practice shots, he could see they had gotten much better. "Wow," he said to them all, "I can see right off I will probably be a loser today!" And they all teed off and for the next few hours got serious about their game. The youngest out of the four drove the golf cart and whirled them around the curves and hills expertly now at breakneck speed, their gray hair flying around their visors and whiskers aglow in the sunshine.

As they took a break before starting the next nine holes, they all sat in the cart and watched for their turn to tee off and had a few minutes to chat.

Jesse asked, "Do all of you live here on the island?"

"Yup, yup," the one in the orange pants said.

Jesse asked curiously, "Are you permanent residents or do you come for the winter months from colder parts of the country?"

"Yup," came the answer from the shortest guy nodding his head and who had a walrus mustache and a bald head. His sun visor had drifted down and almost covered his eyes.

And then Jesse didn't know who to listen to as they all spoke at once, all anxious to add their own two cents.

So he smiled at them and said, "Okay it's time again, so let's see who gets the first "hole in one!" And the colorful group excitedly lined up again for their first shot at it.

At the end of the day, Jesse suggested they all stop at the clubhouse for a celebratory drink.

"But we've only got time for one," The one in the orange pants exclaimed after seeing the rest of the guys nodding their heads eagerly.

"That's good as I should get on the road too," Jesse agreed. And the foursome trouped into the lounge where Justin Bieber was extolling the virtues of staying single on a sound system to this somewhat aged crowd. Jesse remembered his son Jesse Junior playing this over and over on his stereo and for a while he was saddened by things not being as they used to be.

Their drink orders ranged from CC and seven, vodka sour, to whiskey and water. After the drinks came he saw that they were all glancing at him worriedly, and realized they were apparently looking to him to be the leader here too.

"Okay," he said, "let's all relax with our drinks after a hard day on the course." And they all sat back. A little time later he asked again, making conversation, "Did you fellas say you're from around here?"

"Yup," the one with the walrus mustache volunteered again.

"Are you all single?" He winked and went on, "I mean do you date?"

Well, this caused all three to chortle. "There are some available, I'd say." Orange pants replied.

"Do any of you like to fish?" Jesse asked to change the subject.

They all nodded their heads in unison.

"Do you guys have any fishing equipment then?" He asked.

Sadly all three guys shook their heads. "But maybe we could get some," the tall third one said, his eyes growing large as if he just had an idea.

"How?" The other two guys wondered and Jesse looked on interestedly.

"I've got some money tidied away. We could buy some!" He told the group.

"For sure?" the two asked.

"Hell yeah. I didn't have any kids and I can't take it with me!"

"Well Jesse," orange pants asked excitedly and the other two looked on. "Would you help us shop for some things?"

"Of course, I'll be glad to. But you guys will have to make a list because I don't know what you need here to ocean fish with."

And all three senior citizens shook their heads excitedly, and then hurried off for their ride.

Jesse had a good day with his old friends and went to his hotel and showered and changed clothes. This evening he figured he might get a sandwich at Shirlee's and listen to a few of her tunes and then hit the hay for an early night. The fresh ocean air had a lulling effect on him and he had been sleeping like a baby since getting to Hilton Head and another reason why he liked the place.

The café was busy when Jesse got there, Shirlee was at her baby grand singing a Barbra Streisand medley for her dinner guests and the place was humming with business as usual.

At the end of her set, Shirlee came over and greeted Jesse. He had put on a white cotton summer sweater with a v-neckline and charcoal slacks. And by now, he had joined the vast crowd of mover and shakers and tossed his socks back in the suitcase as now it was considered hip to go barefoot in your loafers.

"Jesse," Shirlee exclaimed, "every time I see you, you seem to become more handsome!"

"Really?" Well, then I need to keep stopping in here." They were at the bar and the bartender slid a Kentucky Bourbon over to him and then a tall glass of water for Shirlee. They toasted each other and then sipped their drinks.

Shirlee smiled at him, and then asked, "Jesse, I'm having some friends over to my house for cocktails later tonight, would you like to join us?"

And of course, Jesse had no constraints on his time so he said "yes, he'd like that very much!"

Now as he drove up to the address his GPS brought him to, he was not surprised to see the elegant southern plantation style, two story home, behind a tall wrought iron fence which was open tonight. But a guard stood at the gate and asked for a name before letting him in. He drove up on a bricked circular driveway and another man parked his car. He saw an assortment of late model cars, both foreign and local. Then he rang the doorbell and stepped in to Shirlee's home.

She hurried over and hugged him. "I was hoping you'd come Jesse. Come on in, it's just a small group of my friends and we're having margaritas and pizzas."

Right off, he saw her home was beautifully done in colors of gray, black and white, the accent color of apple green jumped out at you and made you smile. Huge beautiful abstract art on the walls used the same colors and was framed in black. When Jesse exclaimed later about her collection that adorned her rooms, Shirlee exclaimed she'd commissioned her cousin, the world renowned artist, Del Rey to do these for the house.

Shirlee took his arm and introduced him around as they had come into a large room. There were six other people there. He shook hands and grinned all around, then stopped, surprised when he came to Elle.

"Well, great to see you here Elle." And he took a seat close to hers. But another man next to her on a couch gave him a 'hands off' look and moved closer to her.

Jesse hid an instant uncomplimentary look and turned away. There was just something about the guy he had to admit, that really pissed him off.

He'd figure it out soon, or by God he'd force it
out of him!

-29-

Elle untangled herself from Carl's arms as they stood at her door. She whispered, "I've got to go in. I've got an early appointment in the morning!"

Carl laughed, "I promise I won't stay long, only enough time for us to really get to know each other."

Elle had begun to feel uncomfortable earlier in the evening when Jesse had joined Shirlee's party, when Carl had pointedly acted as her date. But she had only been introduced to him previously and had seen him around in the city. So what was that about?

Elle tried to laugh it off, and he had loosened his arms around her. There was something about his demeanor that sent an alarm to her nerve's ends.

"Thank you, Carl for seeing me home, we'll talk later." And she put the key in her door and went inside and firmly closed the door. She had taken a taxi to Shirlee's party as she did not drive when she imbibed. And now, she was sorry she had let this man drive her home and see where she lived. Putting her purse and jacket in a closet she turned on lights as she made her way into the kitchen, where she got a bottle of water from the refrigerator and a glass and went to relax in the living room.

This was a beautiful room that had a cove ceiling, bead board paneling, cushioned furniture done in various colors of greens, blue and cream with perfect lighting from the lamps. One whole wall held the art work she had inherited with the house. Now as she sat back with her feet up on an ottoman to relax, she sucked in her breath and whispered, no, it can't be! She recounted the number of pictures on the wall and saw another new one had been added.

There was another picture of a clown. And as she studied it she saw it didn't have smiling eyes like the first one, but gleaming anger in this one. Now she was sure someone was coming into her house while she was gone.

What the hell was this about? Should she call the police again? She sipped her water and thought about it, then put together her own plan.

The next day, she carried suitcases out to her car, closed her blinds and after several more trips in and out of her house got in her car and drove away. She stored the car in a garage downtown and took a cab back home, and slipped in quietly at a side door. Now she was going to settle in with her books and computer and see if she could catch whomever was coming into her house to add the artwork to her walls, and why!

The afternoon and evening passed, then another two days and nights and nothing happened. Elle caught up on her reading, and being a sought after journalist, added chapters to an article she was writing for an East coast magazine. She didn't turn on any lights at night but used a night reading lamp with a pin sized beam to read by. She also sat out on the lanai and watched the stars and the moving scene of the ocean. And waited!

-30-

The evening at Shirlee's lovely home was very nice. Jesse had met some of her friends again that he'd been introduced to earlier at her café and then several new ones. Brad and Andrea, a couple who owned a landscaping company in Hilton Head, and Carl, this new man who wanted to make it known to Jesse, that Elle belonged to him. Elle had moved slightly away from the guy as they sat on a couch. When they all gathered in the dining room around a large table for the pizzas, Jesse stood back.

"May I help you in the kitchen, Shirlee?" he volunteered as she hurried back and forth with dishes and supplies.

"Thank you Jesse, that would be lovely. I just need to get some more plates." As he hurried to catch up with her, safely out of hearing, he whispered, "Shirlee, who is that man sitting next to Elle Moore?"

Shirlee stopped and wrinkled her brow. "Oh, do you mean Carl?"

"If that's his name," Jesse remarked drily.

Shirlee took a stack of plates out of a cupboard and handed them to him. Then found napkins and turned to go saying, "He's been around and seems okay. Why?"

"There's something about him," Jesse exclaimed. "I can't put my finger on it, but he seems almost familiar."

"You've met him before somewhere?" Shirlee asked and then they were back in the dining room. He took a chair on the end of the table and quickly ate a piece pepperoni pizza, then stood up saying, "Thank you, Shirlee, for inviting me to your lovely home. I have an early appointment in the morning so I need to leave." He just nodded to the rest of the people at the table and Shirlee walked him to the door. He was pissed that Elle had allowed this man to sit so close to her and act as her date. Well hell, maybe he was!

It was going on midnight as Jesse drove through Hilton Head, and instead of going back to his hotel just yet, he decided to go back to the address where he had seen that white Jeep disappear into; The gated plantation of mansions and up-scale homes right on thc dunes. At least now, he knew police Chief Juel Anderson's investigator was on the case as well.

He'd neglected to check out the cars at Shirlee's earlier as they had been parked on side streets. Now as he sat eyeing the area, several cars zoomed into the locked gate and disappeared.

To Jesse who sat hidden in a copse of pine trees, he was curious as to what kind of cars belonged there. He had been there for over an hour, when suddenly a sea foam green Maserati purred and growled as it also slid in through gates.

Jesse quickly snapped a picture on his cell of the back of it with the license plate number. Whoever was at the wheel was hidden behind darkened windows and it had sailed by so fast that was all Jesse could see. And after another hour he gave it up and went back to his hotel. The next morning he called Reed Conners in Birch Lake.

"Jesse, what do you need?" Reed asked.

"Hey buddy," Jesse said, "have you got a minute? I've got another license and I want to know who this one belongs too!"

"Right, give me a few minutes and I'll call you back."

Jesse stood with a towel tucked around his waist after his shower and brushed his teeth as he waited. There had been several more cars that had vanished into the plantation last night, but the foreign model was the only one that had caught his attention. His cell chirped.

"What did you get?" he asked Reed.

"Listen to this, that plate is registered to a company called "Progress", which is located in California. Nothing more. Nada!"

"What the hell?" Jesse exclaimed.

"Sorry," Reed went on. "If you want me to, I can stay on it and see what comes up."

"Thanks, I'd appreciate that." Jesse finished in the bath room and dialed Elle's number. He'd been irritated at the party last night at Shirlee's house and wanted to ask her who the hell this dude was who seemed to be her date. Hell, he was still pissed! At himself mostly, for just assuming since they had spent those good times together, that something was beginning to blossom between them. Well, God almighty, he was from the "sticks", and apparently things were different here in the cities. He almost clicked off his cell when she answered.

"Good morning," she whispered.

Jesse smoothed out his own voice, "Good morning Elle," he said, "is it too early to call?"

"No, not at all. I'm just having my coffee." She whispered again.

"Elle," Jesse asked, "I need to know. Do you have something going with that dude, Carl something?"

Elle sucked in her breath and raised her voice. "Absolutely not! Jesse, I'm glad you called about this. I was introduced to that man at a restaurant months ago, and have run into him around town several times, but believe me, I've never been out with him!"

"What was going on last night then?" Jesse wanted to know.

Elle was silent for a moment. "You know, he was just sitting there before you came in. And when you were introduced around it was then, when he slid over closer to me."

"Yeah?" Tongue in cheek, Jesse thought about that, and then remarked casually. "Seems like he wanted to prove a point."

"What are you talking about?" Elle asked.

Jesse forced a casual remark. "It's a man thing Elle, egos!"

Elle had neglected to say that she had foolishly taken Carl up on his offer for a ride home after the party broke up. And, that she had to almost forcefully break away from his embrace at her door.

"Would you like to get together later this week?" Jesse asked wanting to know right away.

"I'd love it, Jesse. Let's plan a special night out on the town." Elle suggested. "And believe me, that man means nothing to me!

When Jesse clicked off his cell, he swore. Who the hell was this Carl?

He finished in the bathroom and got ready for another day at a beach. But first, he wanted to catch up with Juel Anderson, the Police Chief of Hilton Head.

"Jesse, just where the hell are you?" She wanted to know.

"I've been moving around. And I'm still sucking air." He added sarcastically.

"I take it then nothing else has happened?" She asked.

"Nope, but I'm wondering, do you have any leads on the murder of that young girl?"

"I'm not at liberty to say Jesse. But I will tell you we've got some individuals we're watching."

"Hmm-, good to know." Jesse was silent for a few seconds. He wondered if he should tell her about the "white Jeep" and his attempts to find the driver. But then he might be way off base and she'd only bitch about his sticking his nose in her investigation. But hell, it could answer a lot of questions. Like, this person could be the murderer of that poor young girl found dead on the beach, and the same psycho who was playing with his life. But maybe later, he decided, and went on to say, "Thanks Chief, let me know if I can help in some way."

"You just stay off the beaches, Jesse, and I need your present address for my notes."

He gave her the one at the last hotel, and not the new one he'd found later.

It was still early in the morning and sunny with a gentle breeze, and an ideal time for the beaches to claim its many occupants. Jesse oiled up and dressed in shorts and a shirt, and covered his head with a new straw visor and some big old fashioned sunglasses. He went back to the beach where the second shooting incident had happened. He sat with his books in a sand chair and studied the crowd behind his large lenses. Several hours had gone by when out of the blue; a lone man came into view. Jesse watched him as he came closer, he was scanning the females sunning on towels and lounges. Jesse raised his book to almost cover his face as he pretended to read. As the man came closer, Jesse saw that he could be the same person he'd seen before who had left the beach with Amy Paulson, the owner of the white jeep. Same height, same walk. A big man.

Jesse's heart banged in his chest as the man passed by, barely ten yards away. He was hidden behind his book except for a slit on top. He watched warily as further down the beach he saw the man turn and go over the dunes and likely to his vehicle.

Jesse jumped up and tossed his books in the bag and ran after him and this time saw the guy climb into an SUV. He had his cell out in time to get the license number and picture as he hurried to his own hidden car in the last row.

God almighty, he exclaimed as he got in his Buick and floored it. As he got close to the first stop light, he could see the SUV waiting to get through. He purposely slowed now and stayed four cars behind him, and followed him back to the same, locked plantation he had been watching last night.

-31-

Elle Moore had her Colt .45 right next to her at all times, and it was late in the day of the third day, when she heard a key in a side door, then heard the door swoosh as it was closed quietly. She had been sitting curled up on the couch in the living room dozing when suddenly her senses were awakened. She clutched her gun and waited. The sun had clouded over and the room was dark, especially with everything closed up. Elle strained to see. She held her gun ready under an afghan that lay across her lap. Then to her amazement a woman crept in clasping a picture to her chest. She was wearing washed out jeans and run down moccasins, and her long black hair clipped up in a pony-tail.

"Stop right there lady, this gun is loaded!" Elle said jumping to her feet.

The woman stiffened and stood still, not moving a muscle.

"Who are you?" Elle yelled at her.

It seemed the woman was at a loss for words and Elle asked again, and finally the stranger spoke.

"Don't shoot me, Mrs. Moore, my name is Mariah." She said and then collapsed on the floor in tears. The picture still clasped in her arms.

"What on earth is going on here, Mariah?" Elle asked, coming to stand by her. Then putting the gun in a pocket Elle reached out a hand. "Come on up and for God's sake and tell me what's going on."

Mariah wiped her tears on her jacket sleeve and stood up. "Mrs. Moore, the paintings are mine and I'm sorry to have come into your house."

"But why?" Elle asked firmly. "Why, this is my house!"

"I needed to hide my art to keep it safe?" Mariah whispered.

"From who?" Elle asked as they both stood in the living room. Then Elle went over and turned on a light which flooded the room. Then she saw Mariah was young and thin. "Come on and sit down," she suggested then. And Mariah backed over to a chair and still held her picture in her lap.

"Why do you need to hide your art, Mariah?" Elle asked again. And she watched as the girl swallowed hard and took a breath.

"My uncle stole my other work. You see I was ready to have a show in a gallery in New York last year." The girl hiccupped and pushed her dark hair off her face. "He broke into my apartment and stole all of it. You see my artwork has become well known and my family wanted to take over."

"Who is your uncle?" Elle asked curiously.

"A real jerk," Mariah whispered and shook her head. "You see, Mrs. Moore, I had been hiding and living in your house before you bought it, and when you did I had no place to put my work."

"You lived in here?" Elle asked.

Mariah nodded. "I had to leave my apartment and I hid out here for months and worked like crazy to put together these pieces for another show."

"Your uncle? Why do you think your uncle would take your work again?" Elle asked.

"You see, they are rich! When he took my paintings before he probably got orders from his grandmother, my great gran who runs the show in the family. I broke away from them awhile back."

"Do you think he knows you're putting together another show?" Elle studied the girl as she talked.

"I'm sure, but he doesn't know I'm still here in Hilton Head and have not gone back home."

"Where is back home?" Elle wanted to know.

"Mrs. Moore, I used to live in Mexico until I became a citizen here in the US. My family is still there."

"Where do you live now?" Elle asked.

"I can't tell you, I'm sorry, but Mrs. Moore," Mariah wailed, "could I please leave my art work here for several more weeks, and then I promise to relieve you of them. I just got confirmation that I will have a show then in New York." Then added, "I'm so sorry I had to scare the daylights out of you with the lights going out those times, and then the car trouble. I was hoping to get you to leave so I could stay here and finish my work." She gulped as she finished. "I'm sorry," she whispered again.

Elle decided to help the girl and said, "Okay, you can finish your work and it'll be safe here with me Mariah. But if you need to come in here from now on, I need to know that. And I will be changing the lock and up-dating my security."

The girl smiled. "Thank you and I promise. May I add this one to the wall then?" And she held out a beautiful piece of art of the ocean at sunset.

After the girl, left Elle poured herself a snifter of brandy and sat out on her lanai. For God's sake, the whole situation seemed like something out of a mystery book. And, she realized she never did get the name of this uncle who had stolen the poor girl's art work.

It was still early in the afternoon and she called her locksmith and asked him to come right over and get started on the changes she needed to do. There also was another reason she wanted this done and that was because of this man called Carl, who she had let drive her home last night. There was just something about him that she didn't like and didn't trust.

-32-

Jesse stopped at the gated plantation and watched the SUV sail in through the locked gate and disappears into the depths of mansions and homes of the rich. He made a U-turn and stopped a block away at a strip mall and made another call to Reed Conners in Birch Lake.

"Reed," he said, "I've got another license number. Have you got time to run it for me again?"

"Yeah, I'm here at the Woodsman Café with the guys. Give me a few minutes after I get through here and I'll get right on it." And Jesse sent the pictures off his cell to Reed.

As Jesse waited for a return call from Reed, he went back to the same gated area and settled down to wait again. There was just something about that green foreign sports car that he had seen earlier that got his curiosity going. As he sat there waiting, he remembered the night before he had ducked back in to the living room at Shirlee's party and grabbed up the glass that Carl, this asshole had been drinking from and stuffed it in his pants pocket. It was a sudden practiced habit that as a sheriff he still couldn't pass up, and he had it under the seat in his Buick. This smooth asshole had irritated him, and he was going to find out who the hell this Carl character was!

Reed got back to him about thirty minutes later.

"Buddy," he said, "get this, that license plate belongs to the same company called Progress that the SUV is registered to, and also located in California. I did find out it's a holding company for an importing and exporting company. That's it!"

"What the hell does that tell us? Nothing!" Jesse said totally disappointed. Then he had another idea. "Listen Reed, I recently got a hold of a glass with some prints I want identified. If I FedEx it to you, could you take it to our guy at the BCA in Bemidji?"

"Hell yes. Do you think it could be important?" Reed asked.

"Might be." Jesse volunteered. He didn't want to go in to the story. "I'll get it off to you today Reed and thanks."

After Jesse got the package off to Reed, he was wiped out. As he drove through downtown Hilton Head, he was sure he was being followed by a silver pickup, a late model four door. But he couldn't be sure if it was one of Elle's cops or if this was for real by someone else. He took them for a ride through side streets and stop signs and it hung close. And here again it had those damn darkened windows so Jesse could not see who the hell it was. But after another few minutes it just disappeared, and finally Jesse dared go back to his place. However, here again he hid his car amongst vehicles in the next block. At his hotel he crashed for eight hours and awoke refreshed.

He went for a run on a trail through pine trees and next to dunes by the water and reached a 2-mile marker. He groaned and turned and started back slowing down and cooling off as he got closer to his hotel. It was still damn hard work but he was getting in the rhythm of exercising and began to like its results. Back at his place he showered, shaved and got into a pair of shorts and a shirt and went back to the golf course. And sure enough his three buddies were there as before and joyously greeted him. Now he knew them as Andy, Herbie and Hank as they rushed to shake his hand.

"We was hoping you would come today," Andy, who had green pants on today exclaimed. "Can we play eighteen holes this time?" He asked as they hustled to gather their bags and go outside.

"Sure, we can," Jesse said and they were all smiles as they lined up to tee off. The afternoon flew by as they finished up, but today they had ended up a little later than usual when they got back to the club house. When they got inside a man met them saying, "are you guys ready for your ride back?" And Andy, Herbie and Hank thanked Jesse profusely and hurried after the guy. As Jesse drove out of the club house parking lot, he saw a small bus ahead of him that discreetly displayed a sign advertising "Johnsons Homes for the Aged" on the side. Then he caught a quick glance inside and recognized his buddies grey heads and caps and visors.

So that's why they were there every time he went. God almighty, Jesse's heart went out to them and he made a vow to keep playing golf with them and see about getting their fishing gear together.

He went back to his place and showered again and went out to find some dinner as he was starved. During the day he had eaten a bag of chips and downed several cokes and now needed real food. As he sat at a stoplight, hungry and thirsty, he really wasn't concentrating on his fellow commuters and to his total surprise a sea foam green sports car flew by.

Jesse's radar shot up and he slid over three lanes as cars honked at his sudden change in directions.

God almighty! He growled, and took off after it four cars behind. Now he had the guy!

-33-

Carlo Prada got his jollies playing this cat and mouse game with that small town yokel, Sheriff Jesse Ortega. He would make this asshole dance until he was ready to take him out. He smirked and thought again, just like Ortega had done to his two brothers, and more than likely his two young cousins who had drowned in his piss lake up there in the fucking back country.

Lately he'd met some women here in Hilton Head who were mature as compared to that prick tease he had run into out on the dunes awhile back. He'd had his fun with her until she'd turned chicken and he had to quiet her down. But he'd been careful about leaving any DNA and was back at his place behind locked gates minutes later.

He wondered where his niece Mariah had gone to. That little bitch was a talented artist and he'd made a bundle on the artwork he'd taken and sold. If he could only find her again he'd put her to work for him. She looked to be a gold mine and he loved every dollar he could get his hands on. He had tons of it coming in from the family, and they didn't need to know that he'd found her earlier and collected what he wanted.

It was going on ten when he got back from a family gathering this evening and he ran into his house for his revolver that he had left at home on his dresser. Usually he always had it with him or in his car, but at the last minute he had decided to leave it home in case he was patted down and searched at his grandmother's house as he never knew about her. Leaving, she had reminded him of her ultimatum again, that he didn't have that much time left to avenge the killer of her sons and grandsons. He knew she would cancel his yearly bonuses from the family's coffers in a minute if he failed to do her bidding.

He was in a bad mood as he left and it took him five minutes inside his house and he was out again speeding in his sea foam green sports car out the gates and onto the streets of Hilton Head. So intent was he on speeding, he didn't see the late model Buick hidden in a stand of pine trees and didn't pay any attention as he headed down town.

He was thinking again of the women he had met lately, especially that bar owner Shirlee, a stunner, even though she seemed pretty up-tight. Then this Elle Moore! Now this woman looked to be a real hot item. He'd seen her around town a few times and then at Shirlee's party, where she'd seemed interested but then when he'd given her a ride home later she'd turned him off cold.

A man of his magnitude! Fuck, he was used to women ready to scratch each other's eyes out for his attention.

Well, he was in the mood for some good whiskey and he knew Shirlee stocked it for her special customers, him being one. Tonight, might be the right time for them to get together, and he didn't plan on waiting around too long for her. He had to admit she had to have some brains as he had heard she'd taken the run down bar and rebuilt it and made it into a multi-million dollar business. Well, he had millions as well, and he didn't work, so who was smarter? He smirked as he spun up to her café, then tossed his car keys to a valet and sauntered in the door.

-34-

Jesse followed the sea foam green, sports car as it sped through the streets of Hilton Head and right into the parking lot at Shirlee's Café. He watched the man go into the café. From there however, Jesse did not have a clear view of the guys feature's except that he looked to be about six plus in height and around two forty in weight. He had a swagger in his gait that irritated Jesse as he watched the man go in the door. He got out of his Buick and started after the man, then stopped abruptly.

Nah, he thought then. Maybe he wouldn't rush in there right after him. And he went back to his car and got in.

God almighty, his heart was still going like a trip hammer so he needed to simmer down and think this through. He hadn't heard back from Reed yet about those prints on that glass, but it had only been a couple of days. Jesse sat for a while, then saw it was soon closing time and decided to leisurely go in for a quick drink.

Inside, the place was standing room only and he edged over to the bar. He caught Dani, the bartender's eye and she quickly slid a Kentucky bourbon over the bar to him. After the first sip of the golden goodness Jesse turned and glanced over the crowd at the bar. He didn't see anyone right off, who might match the likes of the driver of the sports car, but he had never gotten a good look at him either. There must have been several hundred people in all, singles and various groups in the place.

Shirlee did her last number amidst help from the audience then said goodnight and thanked everyone for coming. She saw Jesse over the crowd and waved, then was caught up by her many admirers. He stepped closer to the bar again and winked at Dani, as she made her way over.

"Good to see you, Jesse," she said now as the place quieted down. "Shirlee mentioned that she hadn't seen you for a while."

"Yeah?" Jesse exclaimed. "I've been caught up with golf, I guess." He didn't want to say he had purposely stayed away as he did not want the stalker to follow him there.

Dani looked to be in her early twenties and a beauty. A dainty, curvy slim body, with glorious olive skin, long dark brown hair and the bluest eyes he had ever seen. Jesse couldn't help but shake his head, and then went on to say, "Young lady, if I was twenty years younger, I would chase you for sure." She stood there and grinned and her perfect white teeth sparkled.

"Really?" she said, "I can see why Shirlee likes you. I'd love to hear more, but I've got a ton of glasses to do or I'll be here all night. I've got to study when I get home too." She smiled at Jesse again and began to gather them off the bar rail.

"You're got to study tonight?" He asked as she stacked a tray of used glasses brought in from the waitress as they began to clear tables.

Dani shook her head. "Yes, I've been going to college online."

"Really, I've heard that's possible." As Jesse talked he looked around without being too obvious about it. "What are you studying for?" he asked then.

""I'm just about ready to take the bar exam." She smiled again and took off with her tray loaded down with dozens of glasses.

Jesse took a last swallow of his bourbon and left the café. He hadn't seen anyone that seemed right for person he thought was driving that sports car, and when he got close enough to where it had stood parked just a short time ago, now the space was empty.

God almighty, Jesse grumbled. He headed back to that same locked plantation and found a new place for a stake out. But after several hours, he had to give it up and go back to his hotel.

He let a couple of days go by and spent the time catching up with his reading for real. Actually, he was waiting to hear back from Reed about those prints on the glass he'd picked up at Shirlee's party from this man who called himself Carl, had drank from. Right now he felt things were at a standstill so he went with it. Then the next morning was a Monday and he grabbed his cell as it vibrated in his pocket. He saw it was Reed calling from Minnesota.

"Jesse," Reed Conners said, "I just heard back from my buddy at the BOCA in Bemidji. Listen to this, the DNA showed it matched the samples from the D'Agustino family. They have DNA from all the boys; Mario, Andre and the two cousins that drowned in Birch Lake, and these prints match!"

"Jesus," Jesse breathed. "Who the hell is this then?"

"They didn't have an individual ID of the prints however."

As Jesse talked, the realization dawned on him he was dealing with the same family, the D'Agustino's from Mexico! He had to sit down as his knees tended to buckle.

-35-

As Elle Moore sat watching a movie several nights later she heard a soft knock on a side door. And when she opened it, she saw it was Mariah with another piece of wrapped art clasped protectively in her arms.

"Mariah," Elle said, "Come in."   The girl hesitated for a minute and looked around.

"Is it okay?" she asked.

"Yes, Mariah, I'm just watching an old movie. Have you finished another picture already?"

The pale and tired looking girl smiled. "I've been working on this for a while." And she unwrapped a 16x20 oil painting, this one of an outside scene of a crowd of patrons at a café on a wharf.

"Wow, it's beautiful," Elle murmured as she peered closely at it. "Are these real people here in Hilton Head?"

Mariah set it against the wall and giggled suddenly. "Yes and no."

"Why, what do you mean?" Elle asked

"I like to suggest several real ones just to keep my followers interested."

Elle had to smile at her daring. As she looked at the dozens of faces, both near and far, she wasn't sure she recognized anyone. But then she was new to the area.

Mariah walked over to the gallery of her work in Elle's living room. Her face was aglow with her accomplishments so far and she turned to Elle and suddenly hugged her tightly.

"Mrs. Moore, I can't thank you enough," she said stepping back and turning pink. "Sorry, I don't know what else to say."

"Mariah, I'm so glad to help you out. Like I told you, these pieces are safe here with me." Elle said. "Can you stay for a few minutes and have a bite to eat? I can make a sandwich for you?"

"Oh no," Mariah whispered, "I need to get back and finish. I'm working on my last canvas."

"Congratulations, Mariah. Be careful now and I will look after these for you." And this time Elle hugged her, then closed and locked up after the girl. She turned off the movie and poured a glass of Pinot

Grigio and went out on the lanai. The evening was glorious with a sunset that made you wonder about your own mortality.

Sometime later, her front doorbell chimed. She wasn't expecting anyone this evening and she was hesitant. It chimed again. Getting up and going through her house she peered through the peek hole. And there stood Carl, the guy who had given her a ride home after Shirlee's party. The man who irritated Jesse by giving him the impression she was his date. She hadn't heard from him since then and thought he had gotten the message that she was not interested!

-36-

Jesse had sunk down on the couch in his motel room at Reed's news, that the DNA off the glass he had sent Reed was a match with the much dreaded D'Agustino family. A chill had started in Jesse's shoulders and crawled down his back. As he groaned, God almighty!

"Goddamn Jesse, have you seen any of them around there in Hilton Head?" Reed asked, also shocked at the news.

Jesse was still silent as he thought about this stone cold report, as the startling realization clambered. Thoughts that every law officer dreaded, that someday one of his detainees might come looking for revenge. And here it was!

"Christ, that's who has been taking those shots at me." Jesse growled. "He's playing with me!"

"Jesse, that's got to be it," Reed agreed. "Listen, grab your things and get the hell out of that town, now that we know who is behind those rifle shots, we know he's out for blood."

"Yeah, mine! Wait a minute." Jesse went over and opened the small refrigerator of liquor the hotel had for its guests, and found a miniature bottle of whiskey and downed it. It burned like hell going down, but it gave him a minute.

"You there?" Reed asked.

"Yep." And Jesse said, "Listen to this Reed, this could mean this person from the D'Agustino family could be the murderer of that young girl found on the beach weeks ago!"

"It sounds right, whoever it is, is dangerous!" Jesse could hear the click from Reed's lighter as he lit a cigarette.

"You've got to get in touch with the police chief," Reed suggested.

Jesse's thoughts had been going a mile a minute, and then he said shaking his head, "At this time I've got nothing. So this Carl Rogers is from the D'Agustino tribe. He has changed his name, its cause for wonder, but it's no crime."

"That's true," Reed countered.

"But when I picture this asshole, it was this Carl, the person who was shooting at me. It makes sense."

Jesse ran a hand over his face. "When I think about it, when I was introduced to him at Shirlee's party last week, when I took that glass, I thought he had a familiar look about him, but I didn't put it together. Now I can see the family resemblance."

Reed said, "Buddy, why don't you get in your wheels and hit the road."

"It's a thought," Jesse growled. "But I need to check in to some things first, I'll call you back." And he clicked off his cell. God almighty, he had to warn Elle about this man, who called himself Carl Rogers. That he was dangerous, and that he had probably, killed that young girl found on the beach! Oh Lord, tonight was the night they had planned on another special evening. Then he got the call.

-37-

Elle looked through the peek hole in the front door and saw her visitor was Carl Rogers. It was late in the afternoon, and she had plans of having a relaxing bath, then taking her time to get ready for her night out with Jesse. Now, why was that man at her door? She thought irritated. He should have gotten the message that I didn't want to be involved with him!

She stepped back quietly from the door as the bell chimed again and this time longer. Now she was glad she had put that one sided tape on the little glass insert so that the person out there could not see any movement from inside. But even though she knew Carl couldn't see her, she got chills after seeing the callous look he had on his face. She was wearing a lounging robe that had big pockets and her right hand was closed around her gun as she tiptoed back into the living room. Then realized the patio doors were open out to the lanai, and someone determined enough could scale the eight foot high concrete fence and get in. She ran over and locked her glass doors and pulled the drapes. By now Elle's hands were shaking and she dialed Jesse for help. She whispered, "Jesse, remember that man Carl, from Shirlee's party? He's at my door ringing the hell out of my doorbell. Oh God, now he's pounding on the door!"

Jesse had just put his cell phone down after Reed's call. "Elle," he said, "don't let him know you're home. I'll be there in ten minutes!"

It had just started to grow dark and luckily she had not turned on any lights yet. And finally, to her relief it became silent. She sat still for a few minutes and listened.

There he's gone, she breathed and tiptoed over and lifted a corner of the kitchen blind and looked out to the street. But his car was still out there, the same green Maserati he'd given her a ride home in, from that night of Shirlee's party. She closed the corner of the blind and went in to the living room and peeked through that window, all the while waiting to hear his car start as he drove away. But she heard nothing!

Where the hell was he?

She sat down in the corner of the couch, one hand clutching the gun. Maybe she should rush to the door and look around outside and pretend she'd been busy downstairs. Then she might see what the hell he was out there doing now? No, maybe not. Fearing it was too late to act surprised she sat still as stone and waited and watched. But now that she had the new security system in and new locks on the doors and windows, she should feel secure as the lock and key company promised. Then to her astonishment and panic, she heard a soft rustle at her front door and saw it open and Carl step in.

How had he gotten past the new locks? He stood for a minute in the darkened foyer and looked around, apparently to get his bearings, then came in to the living room.

When Elle had heard the door open she hastily slipped behind the couch and hid. She didn't want to have a gun battle with the man unless she was forced into it. Peeking out from her hiding place she saw him come into the living room, then stop abruptly. Moonlight brightened the area. He swore as he stared at the wall covered with art. He had come face to face with Mariah's art work displayed. 'The bitch has been here all along!' He said out loud.

Then Elle realized Carl Rogers was Mariah's feared uncle!

She peeked around a corner of the couch again and watched him as he stood and counted the art work, then took out his cell and made a call.

"Slick," he said, "Bring that pickup truck of yours over to this address. Right now!"

"Right now hurry, she's not home!" he repeated. "I'll have things ready to be loaded. Throw in those quilts." And Carl clicked off his cell and lit a cigarette, then tossed the match on the carpet.

Elle had to put a hand over her mouth to stop herself from yelling at him. But she could see the match was safely out.

She had to call 911, but the man would hear her if she even moved and fumbled in her pocket for her own cell.

Minutes went by as Carl Rogers smiled apparently adding up the tens of thousands of dollars he could get out there on the market for all this art, his sneaky niece had made just for him again. These were his!

And where the hell was that bitch, Elle Moore? Apparently they've been in cahoots all along, he growled.

-38-

Jesse ran out and climbed in the Buick after he got the message from Elle that Carl Rogers was at her door ringing the hell out of her doorbell. And he had just talked to Reed Conners, and found out that the man who called himself Carl Rogers was really someone from the D'Agustino family who resided just over the southern border in Mexico. Thank God, he'd had the idea to send off that glass the man had drank out off at Shirlee's party. He called Elle back and left a message on her voice mail that he'd be there in a few minutes," and careened around corners and even through red lights when it was safe. He also called Police Chief, Juel Anderson. When he got through to her he talked fast.

"Chief," he said, "Hurry, over to this address." Breathless, as he spun around a corner, he went on to say, "the man who has been shooting at me, and I'm betting on, is the one who killed that girl on the beach, right now is trying to break down a woman's door!"

"Jesse, slow down, how do you know this?" She asked calmly.

"Chief, I had a glass he drank out off checked for prints." Jesse was just a block from Elle's house.

"You did what? Jesse, I told you to stay out of this, you don't have jurisdiction here in South Carolina!"

"Yeah, sorry I had to do it. I'm just about at the woman's house, and you should get here now!" And he tossed the cell down on the car seat. As he got to Elle's house, the sea foam green sports car, the Maserati that he had been chasing around town stood in her driveway. God almighty, he exclaimed under his breath.

He drove down several houses and parked, then got out quietly and closed his car door. Her house was dark. Holding the .38 down at his side, he walked around the back to her high fence, and saw that unless someone had a ladder it would be almost impossible to get over it. He crept quietly around to the front, stooping down under windows, and when he got to the front door, he turned the knob and it opened.

Standing off to the side, Jesse pushed the door open further, slowly, the .38 pointed and ready. The foyer was dark and empty, and then as he stepped quietly into the living room he saw a man in the shadows. The man had his back to him and was totally unaware that Jesse stood a few feet from him with a gun pointed at him.

Then to Jesse's surprise the man went up to the wall of pictures there in Elle's living room and began to take one down.

A fucking robbery, Jesse thought. "Hands over your head, asshole, I've got a gun pointed right at your head!" Jesse yelled.

Then to his complete surprise Elle stood up from behind the couch. And in the moment it took for the astonished Jesse to assess the situation, the man flew out the door, and jumped into his sports car that was parked right next to the outside steps. Jesse was seconds behind him and got off several shots that hit and shattered the window on the driver's side of the Maserati before it disappeared, speeding down the street. Just then, Chief of Police, Juel Anderson pulled up with lights flashing on her vehicle.

Jesse had quickly slipped the .38 in his waistband under his shirt and hoped she hadn't seen it or heard the shots.

"What the hell is going on, Jesse?" the chief shouted getting out of her patrol car and coming over.

"You can't just call me and order me to drop everything and get right over to an address!"

By now, Elle Moore stood just inside the doorway and saw and heard the commotion. She stepped out and said, "I'm Elle Moore and I live here." Her face was ashen as she went on. "Would you like to come in, and I can explain."

"Thank you, Miss Moore. I am Juel Anderson, the Chief of Police here in Hilton Head. And yes, I would like to know what is going on here! Do I smell gun powder?" And she glared at Jesse as the three went inside and Elle lead them into the living room.

"First of all," Jesse said, still standing as the two women sat down on facing davenports. "I told you that this man's fingerprints match those from a family with whom I've had prior dealings with."

"And where is this man now?" The chief asked.

Jesse paced around the room. "He took off," he growled.

"Let me start at the beginning," Elle spoke up. She pointed to the many pieces of art on her walls. "I have been keeping these art pieces safe for Mariah, a friend, who has been getting ready for a gallery show in New York. Because she had told me about this man, her uncle, who had stolen her complete collection a few years ago. It was a coincidence that I had met this same man, and that I had her art here. I saw his complete surprise when he came face to face and recognized her work."

"Why did he break in, in the first place?"

Elle grimaced, "Oh damn, I'd met him around town a few times and accepted a ride home from him one time when we happened to both be at the same party. I brushed his advances off at my door and I think he got angry. I don't know why he came over tonight but, I felt like he knew I was home. And when I didn't answer the door, he just broke in to see why." Elle sat with her arms clasped protectively around her chest. "If he hadn't seen Mariah's art work here, I wonder what he might have had in mind."

"You're probably very lucky, Mrs. Moore." Chief Anderson looked around the lovely expensively furnished room. "You had your doors locked?" She asked.

"Of course, and I just had a new security system installed. How did he get in?" Elle shook her head. And as she sat, she pulled the pink silk robe tighter around herself.

"Miss Moore," the chief said standing up. "I've got your report, and I would suggest that you call someone to come over, or better yet, stay somewhere else tonight." Juel Anderson reached over and put reassuring hand on Elle's shoulder. "Rest assured, I will find out who this character is and bring him down!" Elle stood up then too and said a weak "thank you." "And Mr. Ortega," the chief ordered, "you need to come down to my office right now!" And she left.

Ah hell, Jesse thought, he could have been right behind that asshole in the green sports car. Now he had to waste hours explaining everything to the chief of police.

He took Elle's hand. "Run and put on some jeans and go down to Shirlee's and I'll meet you there as soon as I can. I'll wait right here now until you are ready."

It took Elle Moore five minutes to throw on some clothes and grab her make-up bag and she was out of there!

-39-

Jesse kept an eye on Elle's Mercedes as she followed him down to Shirlee's Café, then he saw her park and go in and he headed down to the police station.

Damn, he knew Chief Juel would be pissed, not only that he had sent in that glass to be analyzed but also he was sure she could smell the gunpowder still in the air when she had gotten to Elle Moore's home. He slid the .38 under the car seat as he parked and went in to the chief's office. She was at her desk looking very official.

"Mr. Ortega, please have a seat." Her greeting was abrupt as she shuffled some papers around on her desk.

"Thank you," Jesse said and sat down in one of the straight chairs across from her desk. Then he said, "Chief, again I apologize for my urgent call to you. I needed help!"

"I got that, Mr. Ortega. First of all, do you want to share with me the identity of this person you think is behind shooting at you and is also, the murderer of the girl found on the beach?" Juel Anderson leaned over close in his face.

Jesse didn't flinch and said, "Chief, first I need to bring you up on a case I had years ago back in Birch Lake, MN when I was a sheriff. A former resident got mixed up with a notorious drug dealer. She saw him shoot a man while out on the ocean and then toss the body overboard. The FBI got involved, there was a trial, and in the end I had two brothers and two young gays all dead in my town. All four are from the D'Agustino family, which now we know live right across your border."

Chief Anderson nodded. "Yes, I'm aware of them. Now tell me about the DNA results from the fingerprints on that glass that you somehow orchestrated?" Her eyes held his. "You didn't have authorization to do that!"

"But God almighty, I felt it was important." Jesse slammed his fist on the desk. "Chief, there was something about that man that got my attention."

"Well, you might as well tell me. What did you find out?"

Jesse swallowed. "Listen to this, the DNA from the glass matched the DNA the Bureau Of Criminal Apprehensions has on record belonging to the D'Agustino family." He sat back and ran a hand over his face.

Juel Anderson sat still for a moment. "Okay Jesse, you may as well tell me everything you have pertaining to this case. So you think, this man is the same one who has been taunting you with those rifle shots, the man who killed the girl too? "

"Chief I know so, alright I will admit I have been following the man. I know where he lives and that his DMV is registered to a company that lists exports and imports. You know that the D'Agustino's are one of the biggest drug suppliers in the world, don't you?" Jesse exclaimed. His face was red.

Chief Juel Anderson had a closed look on her face. "Jesse, we've always known who they are. Now tell me, why do you think someone from there is responsible for stalking you?"

Jesse sat up and cleared his throat. "Well, it just makes sense to me that the family has caught up with me here. You see, they think I killed their family members."

"Did you?" The chief asked with an apprehensive look in her eyes.

"No, not personally, but Mario and Andre D'Agustino forced us into a gun battle. And they both had the misfortune of getting killed. The two young gay men apparently had a falling out with each other, and as near as we could figure out it was a double suicide."

"You said the FBI was there?"

Jesse shrugged his shoulders. "And, we were lucky; if they hadn't been we'd probably been wiped off the map!" He was tired of it all. Suddenly this place didn't feel as good as it had.

"What happened today inside Miss Moore's house?" The chief asked then.

"Elle called me and she was scared. She said this man whom she'd met several times, was at her door and wouldn't stop ringing her doorbell, and leave. She asked for help and when I got there the door was open. I stepped in quietly and saw this man was standing in the living room, his back to me. He seemed to be studying something on the living wall. Then I saw him go over to this wall which was covered with oil paintings and began to take one down. I thought it was a robbery and I stopped him!"

"How?" She asked.

"I had my gun pointed at his head," Jesse finally volunteered. Then he went on, "Chief, it was the stalker, the man who has been shooting at me. I want him arrested!"

She studied Jesse while running a hand over her face.

Jesse stood up. "Chief, keep in mind this man could be the murderer too!"

Later, undaunted, sitting in his car outside the police station, he took out his cell and went online and searched for any news articles about the D'Agustino family. Not surprisingly, there were not many. He did learn there were three families, the D'Agustino's, Mercado's and the Prada's. The offspring of these three original families ran the huge enterprises which consisted of imports and exports, real estate, and banks. There were few pictures available, but Jesse studied the face of one man who looked to be in his thirties.

God almighty, he slammed a fist into the steering wheel. "This is the one!" And he climbed out of the Buick and retraced his steps back to Chief Juel Anderson's office. She was on the phone and put a hand up.

After a few minutes, she hung up the phone. "What's up Jesse?"

"I just went to the internet and guess what? I found the face I just saw in Elle's living room."

"Show me!" Juel Anderson calmly turned to her computer. After searching she found the same site and began flipping through pages. "Okay, here's one with some of the families. Do you recognize anyone from here?" And she turned to the same page Jesse had found only now on her bigger screen.

"Here," he said and pointed to a young man who stared back defiantly at the camera. "That's the man! That's the one who was in Elle's house. And that's the man who has been shooting at me. And he could also be that young girl's killer!"

Chief Anderson's face paled and Jesse could see she swallowed hard. After a minute she exclaimed "Jesus Christ" under her breath. "That's Carlo Prada," she said.

"I want this man, Carlo Prada charged with attempted murder, mine!" It was Jesse's turn to exclaim. "Chief, get a warrant for his arrest!" He yelled out of patience.

Juel Anderson shook her head slowly. "Jesse, it's not that easy. I need to make some phone calls first."

"Why?" Jesse exploded.

"Calm down, and think about this first. I can't just rush in and charge that one of their golden family members is guilty of stalking and murder!"

"Yeah, why not?"

"Because, as you well know Jesse, where's the proof? However, I do believe, that you believe this man is responsible for those charges."

"And Elle Moore will press charges for breaking and entering," Jesse reminded her.

"No, I haven't forgotten. However, I need to work on this, Jesse, that'll be all for now."

And he was dismissed. And, any thoughts he might have had, of another date with the beautiful chief was extinguished right there, he swore under his breath.

He left the police station, pissed. But then after a few choice words he had to give her credit. As infamous as the D'Agustino family was, she had informed him they owned a huge area of real estate and paid high taxes in Hilton Head. And, they also supported the many venues of businesses with their presence and riches. And now settling down, Jesse knew she had to step carefully around them and not rush in until she had some concrete evidence. He drove down to Shirlee's Café and found Elle at the bar talking to Shirlee.

Should he tell them that the man who called himself Carl Rogers was really Carlo Prada? A rich, sociopath playboy who was also a murderer?

-40-

On the phone, Chief Anderson got confirmation from the BCA that the fingerprints on that glass that Reed Conners had sent in matched those of the D'Agustino family. It would be enough to get a warrant for Carlo Prada's arrest for breaking and entering with attempt to rob.

But was she ready to start off an uprising with the family? It had been a few years since she had taken over the office here in Hilton Head, SC and had kept the peace between her town and theirs. And she wasn't anxious to start now, but if someone from the notorious family had killed one of her residents and was stalking another with attempt, she had to take action. She talked to a judge in Hilton Head who turned down issuing a warrant, but that was no surprise as she knew he enjoyed vacationing in Mexico. So for now she was on her own. She got in her official car and at the gate to the D'Agustino estates a uniformed man stepped out of the enclosure.

"Chief Anderson, to what do I owe for this pleasant surprise?" He asked and the man's muscle bound body stretched his shirt taut. He came over to her car.

"Alex, direct me to Carlo Prada's place, would you please?" Juel had known Alex since they had both been kids.

"Sorry, I can't do that Chief. I got orders you know."

Juel smiled at him. "Now Alex," she said patiently, "I'm the law around here and that means what I say, goes! Open that gate now or I will drive right through it!"

"Chief, don't make me lose this job." Alex stepped back and his muscles bulged, but his baby face looked scared.

The chief didn't have time for this. She took her foot off the brake, pressed on the gas and her vehicle crashed through the gate as Alex stood bewildered. She had Prada's address in her pocket and took it out now and glanced around for the place.

At his door she rang the doorbell and stood and waited, knowing by now Alex, the gatekeeper would have alerted him. She held her right hand down at her side, ready to draw her service revolver if needed. She had to handle this case with care.

After a good five minutes, she heard someone on the other side of the door and then it opened.

Carlo Prada stood there in a robe. "Sorry, I just got out of the pool. Can I help you?"

She held up her shield. "Mr. Prada, I'm sure by now you know I'm Juel Anderson, the Chief of Police here in Hilton Head."

The man smiled. "Of course I've heard of you. What can I do for you?"

"Mr. Prada, I would like you to come down to my office, you may follow me in your car if you'd like, or else I'll send one for you."

He laughed, "Whatever for?" He hadn't invited her in and looked out at the street apparently to see if her deputies were along.

"A friendly little chat. Now, if you refuse I can get a warrant to bring you in."

"A warrant, Jesus Christ! What the hell for?" He laughed again. "I think I need more information, Chief?"

"Here's what you need to know; this is very serious and we'll discuss it down at headquarters. It'll go easier on you if you come in willingly. I'll expect to see you in thirty minutes!" And Chief Anderson turned and went back to her car.

Five minutes later, Carlo Prada was in his car, but he was not going down to the police headquarters, he was going to get that art his niece had stored at Elle Moore's house. As earlier he had just gotten a call from a customer in his home country, who would pay big money for this collection done by Mariah Mercado, a Latino artist. Anyway, he was getting fucking tired of playing cat and mouse with that backwoods sheriff, but now, he probably wouldn't get the chance to kill him as he had promised his grandmother.

He knew Elle Moore's address and as he drove by, he saw the house was dark so apparently she was out. This was going to be too easy. He'd left the green Maserati in the garage and took one of the many SUV's the family had gassed up and ready. Thanks to a friend who was a computer whiz and for a price, Prada knew all Elle Moore's new secret security codes again for her house. He quietly opened the door that lead into her foyer and stepped into her house.

In her living room he began to take down the art, smirking at the naiveté that people believed locks could keep them and theirs safe. He had several paintings in his hands, when he heard, "Okay asshole, put those down and hands in the air!"

Carlo Prada uttered something in Spanish as he dropped the paintings and then whipped out a revolver as he turned and recognizing Jesse, yelled, "Yeah? This is for you fucker, for killing my family!" He aimed at Jesse and pulled the trigger.

Jesse took cover behind a door and yelled back, "You've got two guns pointed at your head now, and one more attempt at us and you're dead!" He was ready to take Carlo Prada out, even if he was from that infamous family.

"I dare you. Don't you know who I am?" And another shot from Prada's gun rang through Elle Moore's living room.

This time his shot splintered the door frame which Jesse stood behind. He felt several splinters pierce his shoulder, and this time Jesse didn't give a damn who this asshole was and aimed carefully. And Carlo Prada doubled over and fell.

-41-

Elle Moore's house was silent after the ear shattering shots rang out, and Carlo Prada lay on the floor. His gun had fallen out of his hand and Jesse kicked it further out of his reach to under a couch. With his gun still pointed at the man on the floor, Jesse walked over and Elle came into the room now with her gun pointed at the man as well.

"Elle, will you call the police chief?" Jesse asked. And when the call went through and she came on the line, Elle handed Jesse the cell and he said. "Chief, I've got Prada here on the floor. He broke into Elle Moore's home again and pulled a gun!"

"Christ Ortega, five minutes!" Juel Anderson yelled and as Elle and Jesse waited for the police, their guns were still pointed at the man on the floor..

After several minutes, an ambulance roared into her driveway, followed by the Chief's official car. Still holding her gun pointed at their prisoner, Elle had backed over to the door and opened it as paramedics rushed in with the Chief right behind. Prada lay on the floor with blood pooling beside him.

"What the hell did you do?" The chief whirled on Jesse.

Jesse and Elle put their guns down and Jesse volunteered. "He had a gun and I had no choice but to protect us both!"

Within minutes the medics had Prada on a stretcher. And when the Chief asked for a quick report, one of them replied, "It doesn't look good."

Chief Juel drew a shuttered breath and exclaimed, "I'll need you both to come down to the station, right now."

"Okay, start at the beginning Mr. Ortega," she said thirty minutes later as they were in her office downtown. "And just because you are a retired sheriff, doesn't mean I will go easy on you!" Jesse saw Elle gape at the news as he had never told anyone else about his past.

"Actually we had gone out to dinner and had come back to Elle's house to enjoy a night cap," Jesse said when Elle spoke up. "We were sitting out in my lanai when Jesse put a finger to his lips motioning for me to be quiet, and tip-toed into the living room."

Jesse went on, "I thought I had heard a door open, and then I saw Carlo Prada come into her house. He walked right over to the art on the living room wall and began to take the paintings down. That's when I warned him to stop and that I had a gun pointed at his head. He turned with a gun in his hand and fired the first shots!"

"First of all, do you have a license for your gun, Mr. Ortega?" She asked.

"Well, not as yet." Jesse replied grudgingly.

Then turning to Elle she asked, "Miss Moore, I trust that you have one?" And Elle found her document in her wallet and handed it over.

Jesse leaned over the edge of her desk, "Chief, this man is the stalker who has been trying to kill me and I want to take action!" His face had turned red. "And, I told you before he's got to be the murderer of that young girl you found on the beach!" They had sat across from the chief's desk in the straight backed chairs and he stood up now as he talked.

Elle had stayed calm. "Chief Anderson, the reason the man broke in was because he was going to steal the paintings off my living room wall. Remember, I told you before I've been keeping this young artist's work safely for her until she's ready for her gallery show. Carlo Prada stole her whole collection once, and, he is her uncle!"

"Who is the artist Miss Moore?"

"Her name is Mariah Mercado," Elle said, "she's been in hiding from this man for months working on a new collection for a show she has coming up in New York."

"This man stole all her work before?"

"Yes," Elle replied. "She's deathly afraid of him!"

Chief Juel Anderson blew out a breath. "First of all, do you know who he is?"

"Big deal, he's a thug who has connections." Jesse said hoarsely.

"Yeah well, that too." The chief answered. "Don't leave town. I'll get in touch with you both."

-42-

Jesse and Elle Moore got in his Buick and drove away from the police station in Hilton Head. Even though they had a lovely dinner much earlier in the evening, now they were too awake after the shooting to call it a night.

"Let's stop at The Diner and have an early breakfast," Jesse suggested and reached over and put his arm over her shoulder as he drove.

Elle was irritated at him and said, "Jesse, why didn't you tell me you had been a sheriff?"

He did a double take at her question. "Well," he shook his head and went on, "sometimes it just makes people standoffish, and besides that part of my life is over," He said.

"But you should have told me," Elle exclaimed.

"Would that have made you feel differently about me?" Jesse asked. He got out of the Buick at The Diner and went to open her door, which gave her time to answer.

She had a tired look on her face when he reached in to help her out. She didn't move but said, "Jesse, I'm sorry but I would like to go right home. I need some time to absorb all this."

Jesse went back to his side of the car and got in. Not knowing what to say, he started the Buick and went back out to the street. Within minutes they were back at her house.

"Do you want me to come in with you to make sure everything is okay?" He asked as he opened her car door again.

"No, as long as that psycho is locked up I'm okay." She began to walk away and he reached for her arm.

"Elle, I'm sorry I wasn't straightforward with you." He went on, "I didn't realize it might be such a concern!"

He walked with her to her door which she unlocked and promptly stepped in. "Jesse, I'll call you." And she gave him a half smile and shut the door.

Well hell, why would it upset her that I used to be the law? Jesse muttered as he got in the Buick and drove away.

The sun was just blasting across the ocean when his cell rang the next morning. He raised his hand and grabbed it off the end table by his bed. His voice rasped with sleep when he answered but when he heard Chief Juel Anderson on the other end, he woke up.

"Are you there Jesse?" she asked.

"I'm here," he said sitting up in the bed.

"I need you to come down to the station right away." She asked.

"Now?" Jesse asked.

"Right now!" And she hung up.

Jesse tossed the covers off and stood up. He checked the time and saw it was going on five a.m. and turned on the shower in the bathroom. Thirty minutes later he was there. He saw right away when he walked in to her office, her jacket was off and she was in shirtsleeves. Empty coffee containers stood on her desk and her shoes lay under it. Her eyes were bloodshot and her face was pale and he could see she'd more than likely been there all night.

***

As earlier that evening, the chief had gone back down to check on Carlo Prada at the hospital. She had been told to go to a waiting room and she would be called as Mr. Prada was being attended to. But after a time, she got up and walked closer when she saw sudden activity going on in his room. Nurses hurried over and someone ran by pushing a cart of mysterious looking objects. Then what seemed like a long time later she caught up with a doctor as he came out of Prada's room.

Hurrying over she exclaimed, "Excuse me please, I'm Police Chief Anderson, can you tell me how Mr. Prada is?"

The exhausted looking doctor couldn't have been more than in his early thirties. His eyes were sad and he shook his head slowly and blew out a breath. "I'm Doctor Reilly, and I'm so sorry, I couldn't save him." He wiped his brow with a handful of tissues he took out of his white coat. "The bullet came too close to his heart and apparently the stress caused it to stop. We couldn't resuscitate him."

The chief's face paled at the news.

He looked around. "Is there anyone here from his family?"

"No, I'll have to contact them." She thanked him for doing what he could for the patient.

But my God, she whispered to herself on the way back to her office, now she had a call to make of great magnitude.

And during the night the phone in her office in downtown Hilton Head SC connected with a very private number across the southern border. And an intense conversation took place between two governing women; Chief of Police, Juel Anderson and Dona Rosaria D'Agustino, matriarch of the large, very powerful D'Agustino, Mercado and Prada families in Monterrey, Mexico.

Carlo Prada, a grandson had been stalking with apparent intent to kill, and, was also suspected to have been the murderer of the young girl found on the beach. But no charges had been filed on either one, due to no concrete evidence. Carlo Prada had been shot during a break-in robbery attempt and later died in a hospital. After the intense long distance conversation, agreements were finally reached to each other's satisfaction.

The chief's voice was hoarse now as she said, "Jesse thanks for coming in. Sit down." She took a breath. "Last evening Carlo Prada died. His heart just stopped and he couldn't be resuscitated."

Jesse had taken a chair opposite her desk. He looked at her now in disbelief, and still angry exclaimed, "And after all those times he's been trying to kill me, he gets off?"

"He's dead Jesse!" The chief shook her head at his outburst.

"And," he continued shouting, "We know God damn well, he killed that girl on the beach, chief!" Jesse stood up and glared at her.

"Jesse, sit down!" And she waited for him to do so and only then went on, "Listen, I had not found any proof that Carlo Prada did it. And I'd had my detectives working day and night on it. He apparently wore plastic gloves and used a condom as we couldn't find any DNA on her. Remember her clothes were missing." The chief took a minute and went on, "It's too late now, and it goes down on record in the murder book as an unsolved."

"I don't believe this." Jesse huffed.

She went on, "Jesse, you shot a man, and he later died. Granted you said it was self-defense in an attempted robbery. But it will go before a grand jury and they will decide if and how you will be charged."

Jesse knew the procedure and was pissed but after a minute he calmed down. "I hope the fucker was hurting when he bit the dust!"

"Jesse, go back to your hotel and I'll let you know when you will be called to come down for your hearing." She gave him a tired nod as he left her office.

He went to his favorite diner and ordered a big breakfast. A week went by. He did not call Elle, to try to make up with her, and he did not go to Shirlee's place. But he walked miles on the beaches now without the fear of rifle shots whirling about his head.

It was a sunny day, late that summer afternoon, when he finally got the summons to appear downtown in their courts. Even though Jesse was thoroughly familiar with the laws he had never been on this side of the fence before.

In a small conference room he faced a judge and was ordered to tell his story. And, in the end, even though Carlo Prada had later died, it was called a justified shooting. And just when Jesse thought he was in the clear, the kind faced judge slapped a five thousand dollar fine on him for firing an unlicensed gun. God almighty, Jesse was still pissed as he walked out of their court house.

And back at his hotel he threw all his belongings in the Buick and left Hilton Head, SC. Where was he going? Jesse Ortega didn't know. Maybe he'd just drive until he felt it was time to stop!

**TO ORDER COPIES OF
THIS BOOK**
Please feel free to contact me through
My e-mail at
lindylewis1@msn.com
Or my website at
Mystery- Novels- Lyn Miller LaCoursiere.com
You can find my books in
Soft cover
Or e-books on
Amazon.com and
NightwritersBooks.com

Lyn Miller LaCoursiere

is an avid reader and loves to travel. She has a large loving family and joyfully jumps on a plane when an invitation arrives. She lives in Minnesota but also spends as much time as possible by the ocean in the south. Her passion is relaxing by water anywhere, ocean, pond or puddle. Lyn has published numerous newspaper articles dealing with life and life's challenges. Her adventures are set in the Midwest.